KU-201-493

'Do you have a boyfriend?' Fay stretched out her fingers and examined her nails.

Swallowing hard, I shook my head. Did people down here ever think about anything but boyfriends?

Fay was only a couple of years older than Kathleen but just being around her sophisticated cousin for five minutes made Kathleen feel like a dumb kid. The prospect of sharing a room with her for the whole summer was bad enough, but Fay seemed determined also to involve Kathleen in a secret life they both knew their parents would disapprove of . . .

MARY DOWNING HAHN is the author of DAPHNE'S BOOK, also published by Corgi Books. A former Art and English teacher, she lives in the USA with her husband and two daughters.

Also by Mary Downing Hahn and published by
Corgi Books

DAPHNE'S BOOK

The Jellyfish Season

MARY DOWNING HAHN

THE JELLYFISH SEASON

A CORGI BOOK 0 552 524522

Originally published in U.S.A. in 1985 by Clarion Books
First publication in Great Britain

PRINTING HISTORY
Corgi edition published 1987

This book is set in 12/14 pt Century Textbook

Corgi Books are published by Transworld Publishers
Ltd., 61–63 Uxbridge Road, Ealing, London W5 5SA,
in Australia by Transworld Publishers (Australia) Pty.
Ltd., 15–23 Helles Avenue, Moorebank, NSW 2170,
and in New Zealand by Transworld Publishers (N.Z.)
Ltd., Cnr. Moselle and Waipareira Avenues,
Henderson, Auckland.

Reproduced, printed and bound in Great Britain by
Hazell Watson & Viney Limited,
Member of the BPCC Group,
Aylesbury, Bucks

For Jim Giblin

1

'I'm not going!' Patsy folded her arms tightly across her chest and glared at Mother and Daddy while I slumped in my chair and poked at the noodles on my plate.

Daddy leaned toward Patsy, fork in hand. 'I'm getting tired of this!' He jabbed the air with his fork, but Patsy didn't even blink. 'Kathleen is going, Mo is going, Rosie is going, your mother is going, and *you* are going. Where your family goes, you go.' He put a forkful of tuna casserole in his mouth. 'I don't want to hear any more about it. Do you understand?'

'But I can stay with Mary Lou Evans all summer. Her mother said I could!' Patsy's voice rose shrilly, and tears gathered in her eyes.

'I don't care what Mrs Evans has to say about it. Your mother and I make the decisions around here.' Daddy's voice rose above Patsy's, drowning out her protests and pleas. 'Now shut your mouth and eat your dinner!'

'How can I eat if I shut my mouth?' Patsy asked in her nastiest voice.

Mo, who was six, snorted into her milk and almost choked, earning her a warning look from Mother, but Daddy brandished his fork at Patsy. 'That's it!' he yelled. 'Go up to your room!'

I nudged Patsy, but it was too late to calm her down. Ignoring me, she stood up so suddenly that her chair crashed to the floor.

'Gladly!' she yelled. 'I can't eat another mouthful of this stuff.'

Glancing at Mother, I saw her sigh and look down at her plate as Patsy stalked out of the room, her back rigid with anger. Up the stairs she stamped. Then the bedroom door slammed shut.

'Pass me the peas, Anne,' Daddy said, his voice loud in the silence. Looking at Mo, he added, 'Maureen, drink your milk.'

'It's not cold anymore,' Mo whined, but she took a sip nonetheless.

'Don't be too hard on Patsy, John,' Mother said as she handed him the peas. 'She's really upset about leaving here.'

'That's life,' Daddy said without looking up from his plate. 'We don't get everything we want. She might as well learn to accept it.'

'But she's only ten years old,' Mother said, her face all soft and worried.

'When I was ten, I was doing a man's work on my father's farm. Kids today expect too much. That's what's wrong with the world.' He continued to eat, his head bent, his fork and knife clicking against the plate.

'Can I be excused?' Mo asked. Like all the rest of us, she'd heard this speech a thousand times.

Satisfying himself that she had eaten everything but the crusts of her peanut butter and jelly sandwich, Daddy nodded. 'Take your plate out to the kitchen, and then go up and get ready for bed. We're leaving for Bay View early in the morning, and I want everybody ready to go. Got that?'

'Yes, Daddy.'

As Mo left the table, Daddy turned his attention to me. 'Finish your dinner,

Kathleen. You'll never fill out if you don't eat more than that.'

Ignoring his reference to my boniness, I stared at the mound of cold, rubbery noodles on my plate. I hoped no one would notice that I'd picked out all the tuna fish already. If he had been in a better mood, I would have told him I wasn't hungry, but, after Patsy's performance, I didn't dare argue with him. Unlike my sister, I don't enjoy causing scenes. Without a word, I began choking down my noodles.

'What's so terrible about going to the beach?' Daddy asked Mother. 'Most kids would jump at the chance to get away from Baltimore for the whole summer.'

'It's hard for them to leave their friends,' Mother said apologetically. 'Especially Patsy. You know how close she and Mary Lou are.'

'She'll make new friends,' Daddy said without a trace of sympathy. 'And she's got Kathleen.' He looked at me just as I swallowed the last of my noodles and nodded approvingly. 'That's better. I hate to see good food wasted. When you grow up and pay for your own groceries, you'll understand.'

Before he could really get going on his

'adult responsibilities' speech, Rosie banged her spoon on her high-chair tray. 'Get down now? Rosie get down?'

Mother turned to her and laughed. 'Look at you, Tootsie, what a mess.' Scooping Rosie out of her high chair, Mother smiled at me. 'Clean up for me, will you, honey? I've got to put this little girl in the bathtub.'

Daddy followed Mother out of the room, leaving his plate for me to carry out into the kitchen. As I filled the sink with hot water, I looked out the window. Across the narrow strip of grass separating our houses, I saw Mrs Evans at her window washing her dishes. She smiled and waved at me, and I waved back, thinking sadly that tomorrow night I would be in Aunt Doris's kitchen, and everything would be different.

I was just as upset as Patsy about moving, but I knew that making a big scene about it wouldn't do any good. The simple truth was we had no place to go but Aunt Doris's house. Since Daddy lost his job at the steel plant last fall, things had gotten worse and worse. Now that his unemployment checks had stopped coming, we couldn't afford to pay the rent on our house.

11

Although Daddy had found a temporary job in Baltimore as a security guard, he wasn't earning enough to support four kids, so he was going to stay in the city with Uncle Ernie, his youngest brother. He was hoping to have enough money by fall to rent a house in our old neighborhood so we could go back to school with our friends.

As Daddy said, we should have been happy to spend a summer at the beach, but there were several things he didn't understand. First of all, Patsy and I were afraid we'd end up staying in Bay View permanently. Good jobs were hard to find, and we didn't see how Daddy was going to save much money in a couple of months.

Even worse, though, was the prospect of sharing a house with Fay, our one and only cousin, the one and only daughter of Uncle Charlie and Aunt Doris. It was impossible to make Daddy understand why Patsy and I hated her. She was so sweet, so pretty, such a lovely girl. How could we dislike her?

Believe me, it wasn't hard. Although Fay was only two years older than I was, she acted as if she were twenty-five instead of fourteen. Just being around her for five minutes made me feel like a dumb little kid. She had a way of looking at me that clearly said, You are so naive, how can I expect you to understand anything?

Worse yet was the difference in our appearance. Fay had the sort of figure you see in *Playboy* magazine while I resembled an overgrown broomstick. The thought of putting on a bathing suit and going to the beach with her did not thrill me.

Sighing loudly, I put the dishes away and started upstairs to see what Patsy was doing. Daddy stopped me when I was halfway up the steps.

'Hey, Gloomy Gus,' he called from the living room, 'tell your mother it's time for that movie she wanted to see.'

Although it was a family joke to call me Gloomy Gus, I was getting tired of it. I hadn't asked to be born with a sad face. It wasn't my fault that my eyebrows curved up and my mouth curved down. So why did they laugh at me all the time? It wasn't fair.

'Are you still standing there?' Daddy's voice broke into my reverie. 'Don't hang around all night daydreaming, Kathleen. Go get your mother.'

I walked slowly up the steps, dragging my hand along the railing. When I got to the top, I saw Mother coming out of Rosie and Mo's room.

'Shh,' she whispered. 'I just got your sisters in bed. Don't wake them up.'

'Daddy wants you,' I mumbled.

'You've got all your things packed, haven't you?' She sounded worried. 'You know Charlie and Ernie will be here early. They expect us to be ready to load the truck.'

'Don't worry. We're all set.' I watched her run down the steps, her red hair floating out behind her.

While I was standing there, the bedroom door opened, and Patsy stuck her head out. 'Can you help me pack, Kathleen?' she asked, frowning so I wouldn't notice her red eyes.

'Sure.' As I followed her into our room, I heard Mother and Daddy laughing. It annoyed me that they could find anything funny about our last night on Madison Street.

2

Earlier in the day, I had packed everything I owned into five brown boxes from the grocery store and stacked them in the middle of the floor. Mother had taken down our curtains and all our pictures, leaving sad little squares of unfaded paint in their place, ghosts of our presence like the smudges and smears our hands had left around the light switch and the doorframes.

While Mother and I had been working, Patsy had dumped the contents of her dresser drawers on the floor, thrown all her clothes on her bed, and heaped piles of dolls and schoolwork on top of them. Then she had ridden away on her bicycle with Mary Lou, promising she'd finish when she got back.

Now, as I surveyed our room, I saw

Patsy hadn't packed a thing. Following my eyes, she blew a big bubble of gum and sucked it slowly back into her mouth.

'Where do we start?' I asked.

Patsy shrugged. 'I don't care.' Stuffing a group of maimed Barbie dolls into a box, she looked at me over her shoulder. 'Tell me again about that time Fay bit you,' she said.

'I've told you that story a million times.' Tossing a heap of socks and underwear into a suitcase, I sighed wearily. I didn't feel like entertaining Patsy. All I wanted to do was go to bed, close my eyes, and get this night over with.

'So tell me. *I* never heard it.' Patsy waggled a frog puppet at me. Like most of her toys, he was missing something. In his case, an eye.

I sighed and began. It was one of those family legends, the kind you tell over and over again, till everybody knows them by heart. 'Well, when I was three and you were one, we went down to Bay View for Easter dinner.'

'And I was wearing that cute little dress with the ruffles, and I didn't have any hair,' Patsy interrupted.

16

I nodded. 'You had a little red fuzz on the top of your head.'

'And Mother used to tape pink ribbons on it so people would know I was a girl.'

'Do you want to tell this story?'

Patsy grinned. 'I just didn't want you to leave me out of it.' Waving the puppet, she said in a froggy voice, 'Go on, go on. What happened next?'

'As soon as Fay saw us, she dragged all her toys into one corner and sat on them. "These are mine. You can't touch them!" ' I pitched my voice into a high whine for Fay, then pushed it through my nose for Aunt Doris. ' "Now, now, Fay play nice and share with your sweet little cousin." But Fay wouldn't. Finally Aunt Doris grabbed a teddy bear and handed it to me. "Kathleen's going to take this home with her to teach you a lesson," she said. So Fay ran up to me and sunk her teeth in my arm. Right here.' I pointed to my upper arm.

Patsy laughed. 'And what was I doing?' We were getting to her favorite part of the story.

I laughed too. 'You were sitting under the kitchen table eating all the candy in Fay's Easter basket.'

'She's hated us ever since!' Patsy was laughing so hard she was snorting.

'Girls!' Mother opened the door and glared at us. 'You'll wake up Mo and Rosie making so much racket.'

Looking around the room, she sagged against the doorframe. 'I thought you were all packed and ready to go.'

'We're doing it right now.' Conscience-stricken, I picked up a handful of paper dolls, most of them armless or legless or both, and dumped them into a box. 'It won't take us long,' I added, scurrying around on all fours and scooping up things.

Mother sighed. 'Didn't I tell you to throw most of this junk away, Patsy?'

Patsy clasped a pile of old schoolwork to her chest and stared at Mother, her eyes wide with indignation. 'This isn't junk. It's my whole life!'

Shaking her head wearily, Mother said, 'Pack it up then and be quick about it.'

As Mother left the room, I wished I could do something to cheer her up. It worried me to see her dragging herself around the house with hardly a smile for anybody.

'Let's go to bed,' I said to Patsy,

shoving the last box toward the middle of the room.

Patsy yawned and kicked off her shoes. 'Good idea,' she said sleepily.

After we got in bed, we could hear Mother and Daddy talking and moving around in the kitchen, still packing from the sound of it. Outside, rain plinked in the gutters, and a car swished past the house, sweeping our ceiling with its headlights. The Johnsons' dog barked at something, the Likowskys' cat probably, and from Mary Lou's house I could hear her brother Paul's stereo set.

'Just think, Kathleen,' Patsy whispered. 'This is the last night we'll ever sleep here.'

I didn't answer. Instead, I lay still and stared at the familiar shape of our window. A breeze ruffled the leaves of the maple tree and hurled a flurry of raindrops against the screen. I didn't want to talk about our last night on Madison Street. I didn't even want to think about it. It made me feel as if I were truly going away forever or, worse yet, dying.

'Are you asleep already?' Patsy hissed.

'No,' I said softly.

'Don't you even care that we're moving?'

19

'Of course I care.'

'You don't act like it.' I heard her bed creak, and I knew she was getting worked up for a big scene. 'You've never said a word about it. You just sit there, like tonight at dinner, and give me these *looks*. Why don't you ever help me out? Why do you always let me get in trouble all by myself?'

'What's the point, Patsy?' I propped myself up on my elbows and stared across the room at her. 'You don't really think we can change anything, do you? They've made up their minds, you know that.'

'But aren't you going to miss this street, our house, our school? We might never come back here. You might never see Donna or Terri. Or *Paul*.' She was sitting up now, waving her arms and gesturing, her voice getting louder. 'Honestly, Kathleen, you make me so mad sometimes! Why do you have to be such a blob of jelly?'

I sighed. 'You just don't understand,' I said weakly, wishing she'd leave me alone.

'Yes, I do,' Patsy said grimly. 'You let everybody walk all over you, Kathleen. What are you going to do when Fay starts bossing you around? Just smile and do whatever she tells you?'

'Of course not!' I tried to sound firm and sure of myself, but I didn't fool Patsy.

'Listen,' she said, 'you and I are going to have to stick together down there. It'll be us two against Fay and Aunt Doris. The Foster sisters. Okay?'

'Okay,' I mumbled, but I wasn't sure I liked the tone of Patsy's voice. I didn't want to fight with Fay all summer. Peace and quiet, that's all I wanted.

'If Fay gives you a hard time,' Patsy added, 'you tell me, and I'll get her for you.'

I nodded in the darkness, but I felt really dumb. What kind of a twelve-year-old girl needs her little sister to take up for her?

'Are you going to say good-bye to Paul tomorrow?' Patsy asked.

'I don't know. Maybe. If I see him,' I whispered.

'Don't be so shy, Kathleen. You'll never get a boyfriend if you're scared to talk to people.' Patsy yawned and continued sleepily. 'I know you like him.'

I frowned across the room at her. 'I just

think he's *nice*, that's all. I don't *like* him, not that way.'

Patsy snorted. 'I'm not going to tell him; I've never said anything to Mary Lou. You can trust *me*, Kathleen.'

Oh, sure, I thought to myself. You'd never tell anybody, Patsy. Oh, no, not you. Out loud, I said, 'I'm pretty tired, Patsy. How about going to sleep?'

She turned over, making a lot of rustling noises. 'Good-night,' she said. 'Sweet dreams about Paul.'

Pulling the sheet over my head, I pressed my face into my pillow. Outside the rain dripped and splashed, and the trees between our house and Paul's swayed and rustled. I fell asleep listening to his stereo.

3

When I woke up, it was still raining. Had it been an ordinary Saturday morning, I would have gone back to sleep, but from downstairs I could hear Daddy and my uncles shoving furniture around.

'Easy, easy,' Daddy shouted, 'that's one of Anne's antiques. Belonged to her grandmother.'

'Don't worry, John. I've got it.' That was Uncle Ernie.

Next I heard a thudding on the stairs, and Patsy ran into the room, lugging Rosie with her. 'Come on, Kathleen, get up!' she yelled. 'Mother wants you to help. I can't take care of Mo and Rosie all by myself.'

From below I heard Daddy say, 'Let go of that, Mo! Get out of the way, will you?'

Then Mo hollered something about

wanting to help, and Patsy ran out of the room in pursuit of Rosie. I stretched and got up, wishing I had more time to lie in bed.

After pulling on my best polo shirt and jeans, I went down to the kitchen. Mother was leaning against the counter near the back door, sipping a cup of tea and watching our furniture go by. She looked as sad as I felt.

Thinking she might want some companionship, I snuggled up next to her and rested my head on her shoulder. 'There goes the couch.' I sighed as Uncle Charlie and Uncle Ernie staggered down the driveway and heaved it into the back of the big U-Haul truck Daddy had rented.

'If only it weren't raining,' Mother said. 'I hope the furniture doesn't get all wet. It might mildew in Charlie's garage.'

'I wish it could all stay right here,' I said. 'And us, too.'

Mother shrugged. 'Wishing doesn't change anything,' she said.

Just then Rosie shrieked and Daddy yelled, 'Kathleen, will you get in here and keep these kids out from under my feet?'

Mother straightened up and tossed her empty paper cup into the trash. 'Go help your father, Kathleen.'

Leaving Mother in the kitchen, I dragged Mo and Rosie out of Daddy's way. 'Where's Patsy?' I asked them.

'She went over to Mary Lou's, but she wouldn't let us come. She made us stay here with grumpy old Daddy.' Mo stuck out her tongue at Daddy as he struggled to get his armchair out the door.

Producing a new coloring book and a box of crayons, I tried to entertain Mo and Rosie till the truck was loaded. When the house was finally empty of everything but dustballs, I volunteered to go get Patsy. I'd seen Paul on his front porch fooling around with one of the bicycles he was forever rebuilding, and I knew it was my last chance to say good-bye to him.

As I ran through the gap in the hedge separating our houses, I almost lost my nerve and went home, but before I could duck back into our yard, Paul saw me.

'Hi, Kath,' he called out. 'All set for the big move?'

I nodded. Nervously shifting my weight from one foot to the other, I asked, 'Is Patsy here?'

'She and Mary Lou are upstairs bawling their eyes out.' He shook his head to flip his hair out of his eyes, a habit I adored. 'What's the matter with you guys anyway? Spending a whole summer at the beach sounds pretty good to me. Swimming every day, soaking up the sun. And that cousin of yours, what's her name – Fay? When she was here last spring, she looked real nice.'

While I tried to think of something awful to say about Fay, Daddy blew the horn on the truck. 'Don't stand there talking all day, Kathleen. Get Patsy. We've got a long drive ahead of us.'

Mortified by Daddy's rudeness, I backed away from Paul, tripped over his toolbox, and kept myself from falling by grabbing hold of the screen door. As I ran upstairs, I could hear Paul laughing.

'Patsy, we have to go!' I shouted at her. 'Daddy's really mad.'

'So what?' Patsy glared at me. 'Let him be mad. He's an old grump.'

Turning away from me, she threw her arms around Mary Lou. 'Promise you'll write to me,' she sobbed.

'I will, I will,' wept Mary Lou. 'You're the one who won't. You'll have so much fun at the beach you'll forget all about me.'

'Patsy, come on!' I pulled her away

from Mary Lou and dragged her toward the stairs. In my haste to get her out of the house, I bumped right into Paul as he was coming through the front door.

'Gee, Kath, take it easy,' he said as I ran past him. 'Hey,' he called after me, 'have a nice summer, and tell that good-looking cousin of yours "Hi" for me.'

Without looking back, I climbed into Uncle Charlie's car and slumped in a corner of the seat. Say 'Hi' to Fay? No way, not a chance. I was glad we were leaving, I was glad I'd never see Paul again. Never, never, never!

Patsy got into the backseat next to Mo and rolled the window down. 'Good-bye, Mary Lou, good-bye!' she yelled. 'We'll be back in time for school, so save me a seat in Mrs Miller's room, okay?'

I glanced at Paul from the corner of my eye as Uncle Charlie pulled out of the driveway, but he had his back to us and was still hard at work on his bicycle.

'Aren't you going to say good-bye to Paul?' Patsy said as we drove past his house, leaving him behind forever.

'Why should I?' I didn't look at Patsy as I said this, but stared at my knees instead, bony even under my jeans.

'Aren't you sad to be leaving him?' she persisted.

I shrugged. 'He's a dope.' I busied myself retying my running shoes while Patsy and Mo called out sad good-byes to almost everything we passed – their elementary school, the Rexall Drugstore, the K-Mart, the movie theater – until Uncle Charlie turned onto the Beltway and left it all behind.

It was a long, gray, boring ride to Bay View. Mother sat in the front seat with Rosie and talked to Uncle Charlie about all sorts of dull things, and Patsy and Mo counted cows and red cars and quarreled most of the time about who had seen what first. Behind us, Daddy and Uncle Ernie came into sight occasionally in the truck, triggering wild outbursts of waving and shouting from Mo and Patsy. Luckily for me, I managed to sleep through most of the trip.

'Wake up, Kathleen!' Mo nudged me hard in the ribs. 'We're almost there!'

I opened my eyes in time to see the faded WELCOME TO BAY VIEW sign at the outskirts of town. In a few minutes we were driving past the beach, dreary and deserted under the cloudy sky. Along the sandy shore, the Chesapeake Bay rolled up in shallow waves, greeny gray and cold. Overhead sea gulls drifted on the wind, circling trash cans and mewing like hungry cats.

'Can we go to the beach?' Patsy leaned over the front seat, appealing to Mother.

'Of course not,' Uncle Charlie spoke up. 'It's raining.'

'So? We're going to get wet anyway. What difference does it make?' Patsy scowled at Uncle Charlie. 'Besides, I was asking *you*,' she said to Mother.

Mother shook her head. 'Not today, sweetie.'

Patsy slumped back in the seat. 'Tomorrow then,' she said. 'Even if it's *snowing*.'

Turning away from the beach, Uncle Charlie drove down a street past small shingled bungalows. On porch rails and clotheslines, bathing suits and towels flapped damply, adding some color to the gray day. Most of the driveways and sidewalks were lined with seashells, and in several yards flowers bloomed brightly in old rowboats.

Finally Uncle Charlie stopped in front of a two-story brown house with a screened porch across the front. 'Here we are,' he said.

'Watch your feet now,' he cautioned as we began climbing out of the car. 'Dorrie waxes the kitchen floor every Saturday, so don't go tracking a lot of mud in with you.'

Preceding us up the steps, he paused and wiped his big work boots thoroughly on the welcome mat, taking care to set us a good example. The door flew open then, and Aunt Doris gave a great shout of welcome. Hugging Mother, she scared Rosie half to death and sent Mo into one of her shy routines.

'Come in, come in,' she bellowed. 'I'll have lunch ready in just a few minutes. I know you must be starved!'

Spotting me, Aunt Doris cried, 'Kathleen! Look at you! Getting prettier every day!' Giving me a rib-cracking squeeze, she added, 'Fay spent the night at her girl friend's house, but she should be home any minute. She's just dying to see you, hon. Oh, I know you two are going to be just like sisters!'

4

As soon as the U-Haul truck pulled into
the driveway, Uncle Charlie dragged
Patsy and me out into the rain and set us
to work carrying boxes inside. 'You two
might as well get your stuff unpacked
while Dorrie's getting lunch together,' he
told us.

With our arms full of our belongings,
Patsy and I followed Aunt Doris upstairs.
'You'll be sharing Fay's room,' she told us
at the top of the steps. 'It's nice and big,
plenty of space for all three of you.'

Opening a door, she paused on the
threshold. 'The double bed is for you-all
and so is that big old bureau against the
wall. You think it'll do?'

We looked at each other and nodded.
'It's fine,' I said.

Aunt Doris smiled. 'The bathroom is

right across the hall, and your mother's going to be sharing the guest room next to you with Mo and Rosie.' Giving us each a pat on the shoulder, she hurried back to the kitchen, leaving us to unpack.

Dumping her boxes in the middle of the floor, Patsy frowned. 'It's like a furniture display in a department store,' she said. 'The kind nobody really lives in.'

'I know.' I gazed at the frilly pink canopy over the white bed, at the matching white desk and bureau, at the dolls and stuffed animals neatly arranged on the little white bookcase, at the fluffy pink rug, and matching pink walls. Mentally I contrasted it with our room back on Madison Street – clothes and toys carpeting the floor, beds never made, mismatched furniture. I didn't see Patsy and me fitting into this house very well.

Opening one of her boxes, Patsy began pulling things out, letting most of them fall on the floor.

As the pile of junk grew, I picked some of it up. 'You better find a place for this stuff,' I said.

'Do you think Aunt Doris expects us to keep everything perfect?' Patsy scowled at me.

Folding some of her T-shirts, I laid them in a drawer. 'We can at least start out neat,' I said.

Patsy huffed as if she thought I was acting like a blob of jelly, but at least she started stuffing socks and underwear into the bureau.

When Aunt Doris called us for lunch, I followed Patsy down to the kitchen and squeezed into my place at the crowded table. As I took the first bite of my tuna-fish sandwich, Aunt Doris leaned toward me.

'I was just telling your mother how much you've grown since the last time I saw you,' she said. 'You're all legs, hon. I bet you're taller than Fay. What do you think, Charlie?'

Uncle Charlie looked at Aunt Doris over the top of his beer can. 'What?' he said.

'Kathleen here. She must be taller than Fay, don't you think?'

Winking at me, he said, 'Oh, she's a regular beanpole.' Then he went back to telling Daddy about the time he caught two dozen bluefish in half an hour. 'I was fighting them off, John. Honest to God, they were jumping right into the boat.'

'A friend of mine got bitten by a blue-fish,' Uncle Ernie said. 'Nearly lost his toe.'

While my father and his brothers swapped stories, I stared at my plate, too angry to eat. How dare Uncle Charlie call me a beanpole? Didn't he have any feelings? The more my uncles and my father laughed and talked, the worse I felt.

'Does Kathleen have a boyfriend yet?' Aunt Doris asked Mother.

'Of course not, Doris. She's only *twelve*.'

Aunt Doris chuckled. 'Fay's had boyfriends since she was old enough to walk. Remember that boy, Charlie? The one who left his bicycle in the driveway all the time, and you backed over it once?'

Stopped in the middle of another man-eating bluefish story, Uncle Charlie looked confused. 'What's that, Dorrie?'

Aunt Doris rolled her eyes at Mother, expressing her opinion of Uncle Charlie. 'You know, that boy Fay used to go with, the short one with the curly hair. His last name was Malloy, I'm sure of that, but I can't remember his first name. Was it Jeff or Joe? Jack maybe. It started with a *J*. I'm sure of *that*.'

'Good lord, Dorrie, how do you expect me to remember the names of all Fay's boyfriends?' Uncle Charlie took a swallow of beer and turned to Daddy. 'I tell you, John, send them off to a convent the minute they start bringing boys home. You'll never get another minute's peace.'

'Oh, we don't need to worry about that for a long time.' Daddy laughed. 'Kathleen's not interested in boys. She'd rather cuddle up with a good book.'

Keeping my head down, I shot a dirty look at Daddy, but he didn't notice. What Uncle Charlie had said earlier was bad enough, but for my own father to sit there and make jokes about me! I was so mad, I could feel my chin wobbling, a sure sign I was about to cry.

'Is something bothering Kathleen?' I heard Aunt Doris ask Mother. 'She looks like she just lost her last friend.'

'Oh, Kathleen always looks like that,' Daddy said. 'Good old Gloomy Gus, that's what we call her.' He reached across the table and ruffled my hair, but I ducked away from his hand.

'You could dress her in black and get her a job as a professional mourner at funerals. She'd have everybody in tears,' Uncle Ernie added.

Clenching my teeth, I twisted my paper napkin into shreds. Why couldn't they all leave me alone?

'Can we be excused?' Patsy said suddenly.

Aunt Doris looked at me, her face worried. 'We didn't hurt your feelings, did we, hon?'

Shaking my head, I pushed my chair back and carried my plate to the sink.

'You have to develop a thick skin if you're going to get along with this bunch,' Aunt Doris said. 'Isn't that right, Anne?'

Mother nodded, but she was too busy coaxing Rosie to drink her milk to pay much attention to anything else.

Upstairs in the privacy of Fay's room, I threw myself down on our bed. 'Why do they always pick on me? Why can't they just leave me alone?' I was crying now. I couldn't help it.

Patsy flopped down next to me. 'It's because you never stand up for yourself. You just sit there and take whatever they dish out. If you got mad and yelled, the way I do, they'd leave you alone.'

'I can't help being tall and skinny. I can't help my face!' I glared at Patsy as if she were somehow to blame.

'Get mad at them, not me.' Patsy stood up and went to the window between our bed and Fay's. 'You can see the bay from here,' she said.

Wiping my eyes, I joined Patsy. Across the backyard, beyond a row of trees and shrubbery, I could see gray water against a gray sky. The breeze was damp and rainy, and it smelled salty, like the bay. A pair of sea gulls swept by, crying mournfully, and I could hear, very faintly, the sound of the waves lapping against the shore.

While I gazed at the sky, Patsy crossed the room and knelt down in front of Fay's bookcase. 'Nancy Drew, Cherry Ames, Trixie Belden, and a bunch of romances. Not one good book.'

Sticking her hand under the bookcase, she felt around and pulled out a pack of cigarettes and an ashtray full of half-smoked butts. 'I bet Aunt Doris doesn't know about these!'

'You better put those back, Patsy. Fay should be home any minute.' I ran to the front window and scanned the street for signs of her, but all I saw was an old man walking a dog.

'So? I'm not scared of her.' As if to prove it, Patsy went to Fay's bureau and examined the cosmetics and perfume bottles neatly arranged in front of the mirror. 'Smell this!' Before I could duck, Patsy sprayed cologne all over me.

Hearing a car stop in front of the house, I looked out the window just in time to see Fay running up the sidewalk. 'Here she comes!'

'Where?' Patsy put the bottle of cologne back in its place and looked out the window. 'I don't see her!'

'That's because she just came in,' I said as the back door slammed.

From all the way upstairs, we heard Aunt Doris say, 'Where have you been, Fay? I told you to be home at noon, and it's after two. Your cousins are just dying to see you.'

A few seconds later, we heard feet pounding up the steps. Stopping to catch her breath, Fay stood in the doorway and stared at us. Her hair, freshly permed, stood out in a fluffy gold halo around her face. She was wearing blue eyeshadow and some kind of orangey pink goop on her face, and her jeans were so tight, I knew she must have to lie down to zip them up. Her T-shirt was tight too, and her chest was even bigger than I remembered.

Fay looked first at Patsy and then at me. Her eyes weren't very friendly, and I wondered if she smelled the cologne Patsy had sprayed all over me. Feeling uneasy, I tried to smile at her, but all I managed was a kind of simper.

'You better not have been fooling around with my stuff,' she said, getting things off to a nice start. 'This is my side of the room, and I don't want you touching anything of mine.' Fay's eyes narrowed and swept over her bureau, her bookcase, her dolls, and stuffed animals as if she were taking a quick inventory of her possessions. Then she sat down on her bed and scowled at us.

'What are you going to do?' Patsy asked scornfully. 'Bite us?' She nudged me and laughed, making me wish I'd never told her that dumb story.

Fay looked at us blankly. Obviously our long-ago Easter visit was not the legend here that it was at home. 'Hands off my things,' she said. 'Or else.'

'I wouldn't touch your junk with a ten-foot pole,' Patsy said.

'I'm glad you get the message.' Fay returned Patsy's scowl.

'Everything you have stinks.' Patsy's eyes glittered dangerously, and I knew she was just itching to get into a real fight with Fay.

'You just smell yourself,' Fay answered coldly.

As Patsy opened her mouth to retaliate, I nudged her. 'Shh!' I hissed. I had hoped things would start off better than this. Now all I wanted to do was keep them from getting worse.

'I'll shut up when I feel like it!' Glaring at me as if I had betrayed her, Patsy stalked across the room, stepping deliberately in the middle of Fay's fluffy little rug. Then, she passed the bookcase, she touched each doll, watching Fay all the while to see what she was going to do. When Fay simply stayed where she was, Patsy went into the bathroom and slammed the door, leaving me alone with my cousin.

5

Just as the silence in the room was becoming unbearable, I heard Fay's bed creak. Glancing in her direction, I saw her staring at me as if she were trying to decide what to make of me. Patsy was definitely an enemy – but was I a friend?

Catching me looking at her, Fay yawned. 'What grade are you going in next year?'

'Eighth.' Feeling uncomfortable, I traced the bumpy design on the bedspread. When my finger found a loose tuft of chenille, I tugged at it. What was I supposed to say next?

Picking up an orange stick, Fay started manicuring her nails. 'You look more like a seventh grader.'

While I tried to think of a suitable reply to this insult, I pulled harder at the

41

chenille and succeeded in unraveling part of the bedspread. Where was Patsy? Why didn't she come back?

'*I'll* be in the tenth grade at Calvert High School,' Fay said, some life and enthusiasm entering her voice for the first time. 'Me and Cindy – she's my best girl friend – are trying out for the pompon squad. We know all the routines already.'

She paused, and I saw Patsy sneak out of the bathroom and run down the stairs. I wanted to jump up and go after her, but I thought that might be rude.

'Do you have a boyfriend?' Fay stretched out her fingers and examined her nails.

Swallowing hard, I shook my head. Did people down here ever think about anything but boyfriends?

'I do.' Fay leaned toward me, her voice dropping to a whisper. 'His name is Joe. He's twenty years old, and he's a sailor.' She paused as if she expected me to say something, to be impressed or envious or shocked.

But I was speechless. Nobody I knew dated twenty-year-old sailors. I couldn't imagine going out with somebody that age.

'Want to see a picture of him?' Fay grabbed her wallet and flipped it open to a color photograph of a sailor. He had dark eyes and the widest grin I'd ever seen. Scrawled across the picture was written, *All My Love to a Swell Girl – Joe.*

'He looks really nice,' I said and then blushed. Why did I always say such stupid things?

'He's wonderful.' Fay kissed the picture and closed her wallet. 'He's stationed at the naval base down at the Point. I met him at the beach on Memorial Day, and we've been going together ever since.'

I nodded and smiled and wondered what Patsy would have to say about all this.

'But there are a couple of things you should know, Kathleen.' Fay stared at me hard, and some of the friendliness went out of her voice. 'He thinks I'm eighteen, so you better not ever tell him I'm only fourteen. You or Patsy. I'll kill you if you do, I swear I will.'

She looked at me so fiercely I almost believed her, but before I could assure her I'd never tell, she leaned toward me again.

'And don't you dare say a word about him to my parents. Daddy would absolutely murder me if he knew I was dating a sailor.'

'I won't say anything. I promise,' I whispered.

'What about Patsy?' Fay's eyes narrowed to slits.

'She won't tell,' I said, but I knew Patsy would do whatever she felt like doing. Nobody could force *her* to keep her mouth shut. Not even if they gagged her.

Fay sighed. 'You-all picked a bad time to move in with us,' she said, looking at me as if I'd planned the whole thing just to mess up her romance with Joe. Then she walked over to her record player and put on a rock album. 'Do you like the Purple Punks?' she yelled above the noise.

'They're okay,' I said.

'They're my favorite group.' Turning the volume all the way up, she began jerking and twitching around the room in time with the music.

'Turn that down!' Uncle Charlie yelled from somewhere downstairs. 'I told you to wear earphones if you want that stuff so loud.'

Making a face in the general direction of her father's voice, Fay jammed the earphones on her head and continued dancing around the room, singing along with music that only she could hear.

Thinking I'd spent more than enough time with my cousin, I stood up and edged toward the door. Catching her eye, I waved and smiled and slipped out of the room. I couldn't wait to tell Patsy what I thought of her for abandoning me.

I found my sister in the living room reading an old *Time* magazine. When she saw me in the doorway, she looked up and grinned. 'Well, did you have a nice chat with Fay?'

'You traitor.' I flopped down beside her. 'I thought you were coming back.'

'I wouldn't call *me* the traitor,' Patsy said. 'You were the one acting all buddy-buddy with her. Did you forget that we were going to stick together against her?'

'I just thought we should try to start out nice. We have to spend the whole summer here, Patsy. I don't want to fight all the time.'

Patsy raised one eyebrow and stared at me. 'Correct me if I'm wrong,' she said sarcastically, 'but I didn't think she was very nice to us. "You better not touch my things," ' Patsy gave a shrill imitation of

Fay. 'She hasn't changed much since she was five years old, Kathleen.'

'But wouldn't it be better just to ignore her or something?'

'You're going to let her walk all over you, aren't you? I *knew* you'd be like this!' Patsy slammed her magazine down on the coffee table and glared at me.

'Do you think she's pretty?' I asked, hoping to return Patsy's full attention to Fay.

Patsy shook her head so violently that her braids flew out and thumped my face. 'All she has are big you-know-whats out to here.' She cupped her hands about a foot away from her skinny chest.

'She has a boyfriend,' I went on. 'He's twenty years old, and he's in the *navy*.'

'Really?' Patsy looked momentarily impressed, but then she added. 'He must be a jerk.'

I shook my head. 'She showed me his picture. He's really good-looking.' Then I remembered and clapped my hand over my mouth. 'Nobody's supposed to know about him, though. Uncle Charlie would murder Fay if he knew she was dating a sailor. I promised her we wouldn't tell.'

'Oh, yeah?' Patsy looked interested,

and I had a feeling she was storing away her new knowledge for future use.

'And there's something else.' I paused to chew on my thumbnail, hoping I could trust Patsy. 'He thinks she's eighteen.' I looked at my sister. 'You won't tell, will you?'

Patsy twisted one braid around her finger and gave me a foxy little grin. 'I'm not a tattletale, you know that.'

I sighed and leaned back against the couch. 'I think Paul likes Fay. He told me to say "Hi" to her.'

'So that's why you wouldn't say goodbye to him!' Patsy bounced on the couch and laughed. 'You do like him, you do!'

'I do not!' I felt my face turn burning red. 'He's a big dope!'

'Kathleen loves Paul, Kathleen loves Paul,' Patsy danced around the room, chanting and laughing.

Furiously, I heaved one of the fancy little sofa pillows at her. 'Shut up!' I yelled 'Shut up!'

Patsy caught the pillow and threw it back, and I grabbed another one and hurled it. Soon the air was full of sofa pillows, and the two of us were shouting and running around, acting like we always did at home.

Just as a pillow hit a lamp and almost knocked it over, Mother appeared in the doorway with Mo and Rosie.

'Girls!' She looked at us and then the room, taking in the scattered pillows and magazines, Patsy's shoes and socks lying in the middle of the floor, and a half-full glass of orange juice on the coffee table. 'Get this cleaned up right now! If your aunt comes back from the store and finds her living room looking like this, she'll be very upset.'

'We were just having a little fun,' Patsy mumbled, but she picked up her shoes and socks and carried the glass out to the kitchen while I straightened up the pillows and magazines.

'We're sorry,' I said to Mother. 'We didn't think.'

She looked at me wearily. 'You're almost thirteen, Kathleen. I expect you to be more sensible.'

Ashamed, I fiddled with the tassel on one of the pillows. 'We didn't wake you up, did we?'

Before Mother could answer, Mo said, 'She was reading me and Rosie a story, but she fell asleep right in the middle of it and now I don't know what happened to Henny Penny.'

'I'll read it later, sweetie,' Mother said. 'I hear Doris coming in with the groceries. Let's go help her, okay?'

Patsy and I weren't alone again with Fay until after dinner. Banishing the three of us to the kitchen to wash the dishes, the adults, with the exception of Mother, went into the living room to watch television. Mother, as usual, was busy putting Mo and Rosie unhappily to bed in their new room.

'I don't know how I'm going to get through this summer,' Fay said as she filled the sink with hot, soapy water. 'At least your father and Uncle Ernie are going back to Baltimore tomorrow so I won't have to listen to their dumb jokes. But the way Mo and Rosie act is absolutely gross. Don't they have any manners at all?'

Patsy scowled at her. 'I wouldn't talk if I were you. They're little so they have an excuse, but you could at least chew with your mouth shut.'

Before Fay could say anything, Patsy added, 'What would Joe think if he saw you sitting there stuffing food in your face like a pig?'

Fay turned to me angrily. 'You told her about Joe already?'

I shrugged and devoted my attention to the glass I was drying. 'She would have found out anyway, wouldn't she?'

'I won't tell anybody,' Patsy said in a snippy little voice.

'You better not!' Fay thrust a hot glass, still dripping, at Patsy. 'Be careful with that,' she said as Patsy fumbled and almost dropped it. 'It's part of a set, and if you break it, you'll be in big trouble!'

'Where did you get it? At your father's gas station?' Patsy asked nastily.

'I swear I'm going to move in with Cindy,' Fay said.

'Do you think we want to live here?' Patsy glared at Fay. 'I hate this place!' Slamming down the glass she'd been drying, Patsy walked away from the sink.

'Come back here!' Fay yelled. 'You haven't finished your share of the dishes!'

Patsy glanced at Fay, her hand on her hip. 'I don't have to do a thing you tell me. I'm not your slave.' Then, with a toss of her head, Patsy sauntered out of the kitchen, once more leaving me alone with Fay.

Plunging her hands in the hot water,

Fay grabbed a plate and scrubbed it fiercely. 'How do you stand her?' she asked me. 'If I had a sister like that, I'd have strangled her years ago, I swear I would have.'

6

After Fay and I finished cleaning up the kitchen, I followed Patsy into the living room. Aunt Doris and Uncle Charlie were watching a car-chase movie that Patsy and I had seen at least three times on cable television, but Daddy and Uncle Ernie were nowhere in sight. When I asked where they were, Aunt Doris told me they'd gone out. From the way she said it, I knew she was annoyed with them for leaving the house.

She was also annoyed with Fay, who was out in the hall talking to Cindy on the phone. Every time Fay raised her voice or laughed, Aunt Doris yelled at her to be quiet.

'How do you expect us to hear the TV with you making so much noise?'

Then Uncle Charlie added, 'Get off that

phone. You've been on it long enough!'

Fay got madder and madder. 'Just a minute!' she shouted. 'I'll be off in a minute!'

Before long, Rosie started crying, and Aunt Doris sprang to her feet. Turning off the television with a snap hard enough to break the knob, she turned to Fay. 'Now see what you've done!' she shouted. 'You woke up the baby. Poor Anne's been up there for hours trying to get those kids to sleep. Don't you ever think about anybody but yourself?'

'I'll talk to you later, Cindy!' Fay slammed the receiver down.

'Where are you going?' Aunt Doris followed her down the hall.

'Out on the back porch where I can have a little privacy!' The screen door slammed, and Aunt Doris started rattling things around in the kitchen.

'Oh, good lord,' Uncle Charlie sighed and turned the television back on, lowering the volume this time.

I yawned and looked at Patsy. 'Aren't you getting tired?'

She nodded. 'Let's go up to bed.'

Saying good-night to Uncle Charlie and getting a grunt in response, we climbed the stairs quietly. A glance at Mother's door showed us that the light was out. Not wanting to risk waking her, we went into Fay's room, undressed, and got into bed.

'I wonder where Daddy and Uncle Ernie went,' Patsy said softly.

'It wasn't very nice of him to go off and leave Mother here by herself. After all, he's going back to Baltimore tomorrow. You'd think he'd want to be with her tonight, not with Uncle Ernie.'

'They probably went to a bar,' Patsy said. 'That's all Uncle Ernie ever does.'

I didn't say anything, but I had a feeling Patsy was right. From what I'd seen of Bay View, there weren't any other places they could go.

'Daddy makes me so mad, Kathleen. I hate him sometimes.' Patsy's voice sounded fierce in the darkness. 'Don't you?'

'You have to try to understand him,' I said slowly, trying to remember all the things I'd been thinking about Daddy lately. 'Getting laid off really upset him. He worked at the steel plant for fifteen years, Patsy, ever since he got out of high school. Just wait. As soon as he gets a good job, he'll be his old self again.'

Patsy propped herself up on her elbows and stared at me. 'But he takes it out on us, Kathleen. Every little thing we do makes him mad. And he yells at Mother, too. It's not fair.'

'I know, but he can't help it.' Uncomfortably I remembered the time I'd come home from school early and found Mother sitting at the kitchen table crying. I could tell that she and Daddy had been fighting. It was in the very air of the house, but she pretended she'd been slicing onions, even though I didn't see a single peel anywhere.

'I wish he wasn't going to live with Uncle Ernie,' Patsy sighed. 'They act so dumb when they get together, like they're teenagers or something. Sometimes I'm scared Daddy will like living with Uncle Ernie so much that he won't want to be married anymore.'

I stared at her, horrified. 'Daddy's not that kind of person. He loves Mother. He'd never do that.'

'Janie Zimmerman never thought her father would do anything like that either,' Patsy said gloomily, 'but you know what happened to him. He ran off with a cashier he met at McDonald's.'

'Oh, Patsy, Daddy's not like Mr Zimmerman!'

'I hope not.' She lay down, and there was a little silence. 'I think it's stopped raining,' she said sleepily. 'Maybe it'll be nice tomorrow, and we can go to the beach.'

Soon the sound of Patsy's breathing told me that she was asleep, but I lay awake, listening to the venetian blinds flapping in the breeze. The streetlight outside the house threw a new pattern of shadows on the ceiling over my head, and I could hear the bay rolling rhythmically against the shore. I wondered if a stranger was lying in my room back home, listening to the sounds that had once been so familiar to me.

Just as I was about to drift off into a dream about Paul, I heard Daddy and Uncle Ernie come home. They made a lot of noise downstairs, laughing and talking. Then Daddy came up the steps, a little unsteadily I thought, and opened the door to Mother's room.

'You awake?' I heard him ask Mother.

'Where have you been?' She sounded

sleepy. Or had she been crying? 'It's after eleven, John.'

'Oh, Ernie wanted to get out of here for a while,' Daddy said. 'This kid stuff really gets to him. He's not used to all the crying and carrying on. Hell, it even gets to me sometimes.'

'Don't wake up Mo and Rosie, honey,' Mother whispered as Daddy's voice rose. 'Just get in bed, okay?'

I heard mumblings and rustlings and Mother saying something about Ernie. 'Don't start that, Anne, not tonight,' Daddy said crossly. Then there was silence, and I held my breath, hoping they weren't going to start quarreling. It didn't take much to set them off.

To my relief, the silence stretched into minutes, and I relaxed, glad that Mother and Daddy had decided not to argue about Uncle Ernie. Closing my eyes, I tried to go to sleep, but I was still awake when Fay tiptoed into our room. She undressed quietly, but, instead of getting into bed, she sat down by the window. Lighting a cigarette, she pressed her face against the screen so she could blow the smoke into the night.

I watched her sleepily and wondered if

she was thinking about Joe. How nice it must be to have a boyfriend, I thought, someone you could really talk to. Dreamily I pictured myself walking down the beach with Paul, sharing my most private thoughts with him. Unlike my mother, he would always have time to listen to me, and he would never tell me the things I worried about were silly. He would even say that he didn't think Fay was pretty after all. 'I prefer intelligent girls,' he would whisper. 'Like you.'

I must have fallen asleep then because the next time I opened my eyes, the room was bright with sunshine. Patsy was gone, but Fay was still sleeping. Lying there, with her mouth half-open, wearing no makeup, her hair all over the pillow, she looked much younger and not nearly so tough.

Not wanting to wake her, I eased out of bed quietly and started getting dressed. As I was pulling my polo shirt over my head, I heard her bed creak.

'What time is it?' Fay asked, her voice heavy with sleep.

I looked at the clock radio. 'It's almost ten o'clock.'

'Already?' She yawned and sat up. 'Smells like Mom's frying bacon.'

Bending to tie my shoes, I saw Fay's feet hit the floor. As I straightened up, I was startled to see her standing naked in front of her bureau, pulling out stuff to wear. Not wanting her to think I was staring at her breasts, I turned away.

'What's the matter?' Fay asked. 'Haven't you ever seen anybody without clothes on?' Squeezing herself into a tube top and a pair of running shorts slit half-way up the side seams, Fay sauntered out of the room ahead of me.

'Well, it's about time you two got up,' Aunt Doris said as we walked into the kitchen. 'Sit down and have some breakfast.'

'I'm not hungry.' Fay leaned against the counter, nibbling a piece of bacon and ignoring the place set for her at the table.

Aunt Doris frowned. 'I spent the whole morning fixing a nice big breakfast for us all to eat together.' She waved a fork at the pancakes and srambled eggs, at the sausage and bacon. 'Now you sit down and eat some, Fay.'

'Oh, Dorrie, leave her alone,' Uncle Charlie said. 'John and Ernie and I certainly aren't going to let anything go to waste.'

Aunt Doris sighed and turned to me. 'How about you, hon? I'm sure you're not always counting calories and going on diets like Fay. You could put on five or six pounds and never know the difference.' She laughed and started piling pancakes on my plate. By the time she handed it to me, the plate was so heavy I almost dropped it.

'Just eat one or two pancakes, Fay,' Aunt Doris pleaded. 'And some of this sausage. It's your favorite kind.'

'I told you I'm not hungry.' Fay glared at her mother. 'If you put it on my plate, it'll just end up in the trash.'

Uncle Ernie looked up from the mound of pancakes he was working his way through. 'Is it like this all the time?'

'Only when they're awake,' Daddy said, getting a big laugh from everybody but us kids. 'Come on, Ern, finish up. If you want to go fishing before we head back to Baltimore, we'd better get a move on.'

As the men crowded out of the kitchen, Patsy turned to Mother. 'Can we go to the beach now?'

'I don't see why not,' Aunt Doris said

before Mother had a chance to answer. 'Just get the kitchen cleaned up first. Then you can all go.' Her eyes swept over us, making it clear that she was including Fay, who was still lounging against the counter.

Patsy and I looked at each other, then at Fay. There was a tense little silence.

'I told Cindy I'd meet her at the snack bar.' Fay slammed her empty juice glass down and glared at her mother.

Aunt Doris nailed Fay with a look I was already beginning to recognize. 'Call Cindy and tell her that you're going with your cousins,' Aunt Doris said firmly. 'You have family obligations, Fay.'

'We don't mind if Fay goes with Cindy,' Patsy said quickly. 'Me and Kathleen can go by ourselves.'

'What about me?' Mo said loudly. 'I want to go too.'

'You can come,' Patsy said to Mo. 'You and me and Kathleen. Wouldn't that be okay?' She turned to Mother imploringly.

'Well, I don't know, Patsy.' Mother hesitated. 'You've never been to this beach before. I think Doris has the right idea about Fay going with you. That is, if it wouldn't ruin Fay's plans.' She looked from us to Fay and then to Aunt Doris as if she were waiting for somebody to tell her what to do.

Of course, Aunt Doris didn't hesitate. 'Fay has all next year to do things with Cindy. While you girls are here' – she paused and smiled at Patsy and Mo and me – 'I expect Fay to spend her time with you.'

Hearing Fay hiss with exasperation, I stared hard at my bare feet. I felt Patsy nudge me, but I didn't look at her or Fay. Instead, I tried to figure out how many days we had to get through before summer ended and we could go back to Baltimore. At least sixty days, I thought. Sixty long days. How would we ever make it?

7

An hour or so later, the four of us left the house. Wearing a purple bathing suit cut low in the front and back, Fay marched ahead of us. Her portable radio was turned up as loud as possible, and she was doing her best to pretend that she wasn't really with us.

Trailing along behind her, Mo and Patsy and I let the gap between us widen. After all, we weren't any more desirous of her company than she was of ours.

'Why are you wearing that T-shirt, Kathleen?' Patsy asked, looking at me curiously.

'I don't want to get sunburned,' I said quickly, glancing down at the oversized Baltimore Colts T-shirt I'd pulled on over my bathing suit. Although it hung halfway to my knees, it didn't hide enough of my long, skinny legs to satisfy me, but at least it covered my shapeless little body.

Patsy looked as if she were about to say something, but Fay had reached the boardwalk and was obviously waiting for us to catch up with her.

'There's something I want you all to know,' Fay said to us. 'I'm meeting Joe at the snack bar, and you better not tell anybody.' She looked at me and added, 'You make sure they keep their mouths shut. Okay?'

Leaving me to take care of things, Fay turned her back and walked away.

'What's she talking about?' Mo asked. 'Who's Joe?'

Ignoring her, Patsy grinned at me. 'So we get to see him! I can hardly wait.'

While Patsy told Mo about Joe, I trudged along behind them, carrying our blanket and a canvas bag heavy with suntan oil and towels. Although it was only eleven thirty, the boards scorched the soles of my bare feet and I had to watch out for splinters.

Gazing across the beach, I watched the Chesapeake roll up lazily against the dirty tan sand streaked with dark oil stains. Out on the horizon, the bay was a deep blue, but near the shore it was a flat greenish brown. It frothed slightly where the tiny waves curled over and broke, sending a feeble ripple of bubbles toward the bits of trash marking the hightide line. Like the water left in the sink after you've washed the pots and pans, it wasn't very inviting.

About a block ahead, I saw the bath-house listing a bit to one side and badly in need of paint. Leaning against it was the snack bar. From its sagging roof, a pair of loudspeakers blasted sunbathers and swimmers with rock music, almost drowning out the cries of the sea gulls circling the overflowing trash cans.

'What a dump,' Patsy said. 'Why couldn't Uncle Charlie live in Ocean City?'

'What's that fence in the water?' Mo pointed at a sagging contrivance of chicken wire and boards surrounding an area two or three times the size of a swimming pool.

'That keeps the jellyfish out,' I told her.

'Fish made out of jelly?' Mo laughed. 'Can we eat them?'

'Sure,' Patsy said. 'Nothing's better

than a peanut butter and jellyfish sandwich.'

'Don't believe her, Mo,' I said. 'They're called that because their bodies look like big blobs of jelly, but they have long tentacles hanging down in the water where you can't see them. If you brush against them, they sting you.'

'Does it hurt?' Mo looked worried.

I nodded. 'If you see one, stay away from it.'

'I'll swim away so fast it won't get me,' Mo said. 'Not even if it chases me.'

When we finally caught up with Fay, she was sitting on her blanket not far from the snack bar. Squinting up at me, she waved a bottle of suntan oil. 'Put lots of this on my back, Kathleen. The sun's really hot, and I burn easily.'

Reluctantly I squirted oil on her shoulders and started rubbing it in. Unlike Patsy and me, Fay was so plump I couldn't feel the bones under skin.

'Want me to put some on you?' Fay asked as I handed her the bottle.

'No, thanks.' Spreading out our blanket, I turned to Patsy. 'Come here so I can rub some sunshield on your back. You know how fair your skin is.'

'I hate that greasy stuff,' Patsy said. Before I could stop her, she ran across the sand toward the water. 'Come on, let's go swimming!'

'Don't forget the jellyfish!' Mo screamed, but she darted after Patsy and splashed in right behind her.

They came up dripping and laughing, shaking water from their hair. 'Aren't you coming, Kathleen?' Patsy shouted. 'It's really nice!'

'Maybe later,' I called to her.

'Come on, Kathleen!' Patsy yelled.

'Kathleen, Kathleen!' Mo shrieked.

Fay raised her head and frowned. 'For Pete's sake, go swimming with them. I'm getting a headache just listening to them chatter.'

I got up slowly, not sure what I was going to do. I didn't want to sit on the beach with Fay, but I didn't want to go into the water either. For one thing, the bay was dirty. And, for another, I couldn't go swimming wearing a T-shirt. If I took it off, Fay would see how dumb I looked in a bathing suit. I could hear her telling Cindy, 'She's almost thirteen and she doesn't have any figure at all. Straight as a stick. A real beanpole, just like Daddy said.'

Noticing my hesitation, Fay said, 'You aren't keeping that T-shirt on, are you?'

'I don't want to get sunburned.'

'I told you I'd rub lotion on you.'

Uncomfortably, I edged away from her, feeling more and more stupid. 'No, this is fine.' I tugged at the hem of the T-shirt as if she were threatening to rip it off.

Fay shrugged. 'If you want to look dumb, go ahead. I sure wouldn't go to the beach wearing something like that.'

Well, I thought to myself, if I looked like you I wouldn't either. Turning my back on her, I walked down to the edge of the water and let the tiny wavelets wash over my feet. Patsy and Mo had given up on me and joined a bunch of kids on a raft. They were rocking it up and down, pushing each other off and laughing and shouting.

I considered swimming out to the raft with my shirt on, but when I was no more than ankle-deep, I lost sight of my toes. The water was too muddy to see the bottom. Who knew what was lurking there, waiting to grab my feet?

Uneasily, I waded back to shore and joined the ranks of old ladies standing sedately at the edge of the water. When

Patsy yelled at me again, I ignored her and made a great pretence of looking for seashells. All that I found, though, were broken pieces. The only whole ones were oyster shells, and they weren't pretty enough to save.

When Patsy and Mo finally came out of the water, they were shivering, and their lips and fingernails were blue. 'I'm starving,' Patsy said through chattering teeth. 'Let's go eat our sandwiches.'

'Oh, look.' Mo pointed at our blanket. 'Is that Joe?'

While the three of us stood at the edge of the water and watched, Joe put his arms around Fay.

'They're kissing! They're kissing!' Mo squealed.

'Shut up, Mo!' I grabbed her arm and gave her a little shake. 'Do you want everybody staring at us?'

'Let go of me!' Mo pulled away and turned to Patsy. 'Come on, let's go up there.'

Before I could stop them, they ran across the beach, kicking sand all over people in their haste to get to the blanket. I would have liked to sneak back to Aunt Doris's house, but I knew I'd get in trouble with Mother if I came home without my sisters.

By the time I caught up with them, they had wedged themselves in between Fay and Joe. 'Look, he has a tattoo!' Mo was telling Patsy.

'Let me see!' Shoving Mo aside, Patsy grabbed Joe's arm. Water dripped from the ends of her braids as she studied the tattoo. 'It's a rose, Kathleen,' she said when she saw me. 'Isn't it beautiful?'

Sitting down on the edge of the blanket farthest away from them, I nodded, too embarrassed by their behavior to say anything.

Joe grinned and held his arm up to get my attention. He flexed his muscles and the petals of the rose quivered as if a breeze were blowing. 'What do you think of that?'

Patsy sucked in her breath. 'Does it hurt to get one of those?'

Joe shrugged. 'Not much.'

'Where did you get it?' Patsy asked.

'This place I used to be stationed. Taiwan,' Joe said. 'You know where that is?'

'Over in Asia someplace.' Patsy smiled at him.

'Smart kid.' He winked at Fay, but she didn't wink back. Or even smile.

'I'm good in geography,' Patsy said, the soul of modesty, as usual.

'I never heard of it till I went there.' Joe flashed his big white teeth at Patsy, Mo, and me, and stretched out his long, tan legs. They were downy with dark hair, I noticed, like Daddy's.

Tweaking one of Patsy's braids, Joe said, 'You're Patsy, aren't you?'

She smiled, obviously pleased that he knew her name. 'Who told you that?'

'Oh, a little bird.' He put his arm around Fay and drew her close to him. 'You're Mo,' he continued, 'and that quiet one over there, looking so serious, that's Kathleen.'

He sent me one of his dazzling smiles, and a million butterflies flew all over inside of my stomach. I wanted to say something funny or clever, but I just sat there sifting sand through my fingers as speechless as I was when Paul talked to me.

'I'm hungry,' Mo said loudly. 'Can we have our sandwiches?'

I looked at Patsy. 'Do you want to eat now?' I whispered.

She nodded and smiled at Joe. 'You can

have half my sandwich if you want. It's peanut butter and jelly, and I made it myself, so it's got gobs and gobs of jelly on it.'

'He can have *all* my sandwich,' Fay said sulkily. 'I'm not hungry.'

'Poor Fay,' Patsy said, taking care to put some distance between herself and her cousin. 'She's trying to lose some weight.'

'She looks great to me just the way she is,' Joe said quickly, giving Fay a big hug. 'I tell you what,' he said to her. 'Why don't you and me go get a soda and a hot dog at the snack bar?'

After shooting a nasty look at Patsy, Fay smiled sweetly at Joe. 'I'd love to,' she said.

'We'll see you guys later,' Joe said, helping Fay to her feet. 'It was real nice meeting you. Keep smiling,' he added, winking at me.

Embarrassed by Fay's scowl, I felt my lips curl into a silly little grin. Bending my head, I traced a pattern in the sand, hoping Joe wouldn't notice the blush I could feel spreading across my face, neck, and chest. I was relieved to see his feet, big and tan, walk out of sight next to Fay's pudgy pink feet.

8

After we finished eating our lunch, we decided to take a walk.

'How much farther do you want to go?' I asked Patsy after a while. The snack bar had dwindled to the size of a dollhouse, and the sun was really hot. My T-shirt clung to my back like a wool blanket.

Patsy pointed down the beach. 'Let's walk to that pier.'

'Can we go out on it?' Mo asked. She was dragging her feet in the water, and I knew she was getting tired. Soon she'd start begging me to carry her.

'Are you sure you can walk that far?' I asked.

'Of course I can.'

'I'm not going to carry you,' I warned her. 'Just remember that.'

For an answer, Mo kicked water all over

me. As I started to splash her back, though, she screamed and ran out of the water. 'Jellyfish! Jellyfish!' she yelled.

She was right. We'd left the net behind a long time ago, and we could see hundreds of them floating just beneath the surface less than a foot from shore. We stared at them in horrified fascination.

'Ooh, ooh, leave it alone,' Mo cried when Patsy managed to lift one out of the water on the end of a stick.

'It's going to get you!' Patsy waved it about while Mo screamed and tried to hide behind me.

Laughing fiendishly, Patsy slung the jellyfish on the sand at my feet. Jumping back, I stared down at the quivering lump; it reminded me of a grotesque fried egg with a blood red center.

'You better not leave it here,' I said to Patsy. 'Look at those tentacles. They're over three feet long. If somebody stepped on it, they'd get a bad sting.'

'We'll bury it,' Patsy said. 'Come on, Mo, and help. It won't bite you.'

Hesitantly Mo approached, flinching with disgust when Patsy threw a handful of wet sand on the jellyfish. 'Oooh, it moved!' she cried. 'Is it still alive?'

74

Patsy shrugged and threw more sand on it.

'Maybe you're hurting it.' Mo looked worried.

'So? Do you think it cares when it stings people?' Patsy went on dumping sand on the jellyfish, and I helped, eager to get the thing buried as quickly as possible. When we had heaped enough sand on it to satisfy Patsy, Mo added an oyster shell for a tomb stone and told the jellyfish to rest in peace.

By now we were close enough to the pier to see that, like everything else in Bay View, it was old and rickety and probably about to collapse.

'Somebody's sitting on the end. See?' Mo pointed at two figures with their arms around each other, hugging and kissing as if they were the only people in the world.

'It's Joe and Fay!' Patsy shouted. 'I knew they were going someplace to make out!'

'Come on.' I grabbed Mo's hand. 'Let's go back before they see us.'

But Patsy was too quick for me. 'No, let's spy on them.' She danced away from me. 'We can sneak up real quietly, and they won't even see us.'

'For Pete's sake, Patsy, haven't you got

75

any sense at all?' Letting Mo pull away from me, I ran after Patsy, but she already had a good head start.

'Wait! Wait!' Mo ran after us. 'Patsy, wait! I'll spy with you!'

Apparently changing her mind about spying, Patsy darted down the pier shrieking, 'Help! Help, Joe! Save us from Kathleen! Don't let her get us!'

Behind her came Mo shrieking, 'Save us from Kathleen! She's a horrible witch. She's going to cook us in the oven and eat us for dinner!'

As they hurled themselves at Joe, I wished that a tidal wave would suddenly rise up from the bay and wash all four of them away. But of course it didn't. Instead, Joe disentangled himself from Fay and tried to escape from Patsy and Mo. 'Hey, what's going on?' he asked.

If Joe was puzzled, Fay was angry. Furiously she jumped to her feet and lunged at Patsy. 'Can't I ever get away from you?' she yelled.

'Help!' Patsy screamed in mock terror and ducked the slap Fay was aiming at her.

At the same moment, Mo jumped in between Patsy and Fay, shouting some of her usual nonsense about witches and goblins. I guess Fay didn't see Mo and lost her balance trying to step around her. At any rate, she toppled off the pier and splashed into the bay. When she popped up, sputtering and screaming, Patsy and Mo howled with laughter, but Joe pushed them out of his way and dove into the water.

'I can't swim, I can't swim!' Fay choked. 'And there's jellyfish everywhere!'

I ran out on the pier, my heart thudding with fright. If the water was over Fay's head, she might drown. My mind raced with images of Joe diving again and again in a vain search for Fay, of the Coast Guard arriving too late to revive her, of our having to break the news to Aunt Doris and Uncle Charlie. I almost had Fay buried when I realized that Patsy and Mo were still laughing.

As I teetered to a stop at the edge of the pier, I saw Fay throw her arms around Joe. 'Save me!' she screamed.

'Take it easy, Fay,' Joe said. 'You're okay. Look, the water's not deep.'

'The jellyfish! The jellyfish!' Fay floundered about frantically. 'There's one, right there! Don't let it sting me! Don't let it sting me!' She was crying now and clinging to Joe like a drowning person. 'Get me out of here!'

Somehow Joe managed to guide her toward the pier and the rickety little ladder. 'Come on, Fay,' he said. 'Just climb up.' He gave her a little boost, but she was still flailing her arms and screaming about the jellyfish.

'She looks like a whale trying to get out of the water,' Patsy howled.

'Whale tail! Whale tail!' Mo shouted. 'Fay is a whale tail!'

'Shut up!' I yelled at them. 'It's not funny.'

Of course they ignored me and continued prancing about the pier, laughing and jeering as Joe struggled to get Fay up the ladder.

As soon as Fay found herself safely on the pier, she leaped to her feet and lunged at Patsy again. 'I hope you're satisfied!' she screamed. 'Thanks to you, I almost drowned!'

'I didn't touch you!' Patsy yelled, her face red with anger and sunburn. 'It wouldn't have happened if you hadn't tried to hit me, you big whale!'

'I could kill you!' Fay swung at Patsy again, but Joe put his arm around her and pulled her away.

'Come on, Fay,' he said. 'Don't act like a kid.' Turning her face up to his, he kissed her so tenderly it made my heart ache. 'You're okay now, honey.'

'But my hair, it's all wet. I must look awful.' Sobbing, Fay hid her face against Joe's chest.

'You look swell,' Joe said softly. Then he turned to Patsy and Mo, who were still laughing and chanting about whales. 'You two get lost for a while,' he said, and his voice was not at all tender. 'There's nothing funny about making somebody cry.'

Patsy froze, but Mo continued capering about, making faces at Fay. 'Are you going to make me?' Patsy glared at Joe.

'Patsy, let's go.' I grabbed her arm, anxious to get her away from Joe before anything worse happened.

'Ouch! Let go of me!' Patsy jerked away.

'Didn't you put suntan lotion on?' Joe stared at Patsy.

Horrified, I realized that Patsy was as red as a steamed crab. 'I told you!' I gasped. 'Why didn't you let me put that stuff on you?'

'What should I do?' Patsy looked as if she were about to cry. 'My skin feels tight all over.'

'I'd go home and soak in a cold tub if I were you,' Joe said, but he didn't sound awfully sympathetic.

'It serves you right!' Fay said. 'I hope you get sun poisoning and have to stay in bed for a month!'

Joe shook his head at Fay and winked at me. 'Get her into a nice cold tub, Smiley,' he said. 'She'll live.' Turning to Fay, he added, 'How about us getting a soda somewhere?'

As they walked away, Patsy stuck her tongue out at Fay's back. 'I hate her,' she said.

'Whale tail! Whale tail!' Mo shouted, but neither Fay nor Joe looked back. He had his arm around her, and he was kissing her as they strolled along the edge of the bay.

9

Aunt Doris was sitting on the porch reading the paper when we came home. 'Oh, you poor thing,' she cried as Patsy crept up the steps whimpering. 'Didn't Kathleen make you put sunshield on?'

Patsy shook her head. 'Where's Mommy?' she wailed.

'She's upstairs, hon, taking a nap with Rosie. Your daddy left about an hour ago, and she's all tired out. You go on up and take a nice long bath. Let your mom sleep.' Aunt Doris ushered Patsy upstairs while I tried to explain about the sunshield.

'I told her to put it on; I *told* her,' I kept saying, despite the fact that nobody was listening to me.

'Daddy's gone?' Mo cried. 'I wanted to kiss him bye-bye. He said he wouldn't leave till I came back. He promised he'd wait!'

Aunt Doris tried to shush Mo, but she wasn't very successful. As we reached the top of the steps, Mother's door opened and she came out into the hall, looking tired and upset.

'Hush, Mo, you'll wake Rosie.' Mother's eyes swept over us and stopped on Patsy. 'Kathleen, I told you not to let her get burned. Didn't you make her use the sunshield?'

'I tried to, but she wouldn't! You know how Patsy is – she never does *anything* I tell her!' I stared at Mother, my eyes brimming with tears. Why did everybody blame me? 'It's not my fault she got sunburned!'

'I thought I could trust you to take a little responsibility, Kathleen.' Mother turned to Mo, who was crying and tugging at her bathrobe. 'Daddy couldn't wait, sweetie. He and Uncle Ernie had to get the truck back.'

'Aren't you going to help me with my bath?' Patsy whimpered. 'There's nothing wrong with Mo. You can talk to her later.'

'Go and lie down, Anne.' Aunt Doris

gave Patsy a none too gentle shove toward the bathroom. 'I'll take care of this one. She's not going to die of sunburn, no matter what she thinks.'

'Let me alone! Don't touch my back!' Patsy ran to Mother. 'I want you to give me my bath, not her!'

'Never mind, Doris, I'll run the tub for her,' Mother said wearily. 'I doubt I'd be able to go back to sleep now.'

Aunt Doris shrugged, but I could tell she didn't approve. 'Don't strain yourself, Anne. Remember what the doctor said.' Frowning at Patsy, she added, 'Somebody around here needs to learn to think about other people.'

'Take Mo downstairs and get her something to drink, Kathleen,' Mother said. 'Thank goodness, you two have your father's skin. Otherwise I'd have three cases of sunburn.' Then she and Patsy went into the bathroom and closed the door, leaving Mo and me to follow Aunt Doris to the kitchen.

'Get some glasses and put ice in them, will you, Kathleen?' Aunt Doris asked.

'Mother isn't sick or anything, is she?' I asked as she poured the lemonade.

For a second she looked puzzled. 'Sick?'

83

I nodded. 'You said the doctor told her to take it easy,' I said.

Aunt Doris laughed. 'Oh, that. It's nothing for you to worry about, hon. She's a little rundown, that's all, and she has to take it easy for a while.' She reached across the table and patted my hand. 'That's why she needs you to help with the kids.'

'I tried to make Patsy use the sunshield,' I mumbled, feeling ashamed of myself for making such a big scene about it with Mother.

'I know.' Aunt Doris smiled at me. 'Just keep the kids out of her hair. Let her get as much rest as she can. You're a sensible kid, Kathleen. I'm sure you'll do your best.'

I nodded, but I wasn't certain I could do what she asked. Surely she'd seen enough of my sisters to know they were pretty hard to control.

'Good heavens,' Aunt Doris said so loudly that both Mo and I jumped. 'Where's Fay? Didn't she come home with you all?'

Before I could stop her, Mo said, 'Her and Joe went somewhere to get a soda, and they wouldn't let us come.'

'Joe?' Aunt Doris frowned. 'Joe who?'

Looking down at the table, I traced a pattern of swirls in the Formica top. 'He's somebody she knew at school. He came along while we were taking a walk, and then they went to the snack bar. She said she'd be home soon.' I felt very uncomfortable as I told Aunt Doris all this, but Fay had made me promise not to tell. What else could I do?

'I never heard her mention anybody by that name,' Aunt Doris said.

Luckily for me, Mo prevented Aunt Doris from asking any more questions by knocking over her glass and sending a cascade of lemonade off the table, into her lap, and onto the floor. By the time we got it cleared up, Aunt Doris seemed to have forgotten all about Joe.

'Let's go see how Patsy's feeling,' I said to Mo as we rinsed our glasses. I was anxious to get her away from Aunt Doris before she brought up Joe again. If she said anything about his tattoo, I knew I was lost.

As soon as Mo and I were alone, I said to her sternly, 'I told you Joe was a secret. Did you forget?'

Mo clapped her hand over her mouth

and stared up at me, her eyes wide. 'Will Fay kill me?'

I shook my head. 'Just don't say another word. Okay?'

Mo nodded. 'I promise.'

'Good.' I smiled at her, hoping I could trust her.

We found Patsy in Mother's room, lying in Mo's bed. The shades were drawn, but she looked very red even in the darkness. I wanted to tell her it was a shame it wasn't Christmas because she could have taken Rudolph's place, but I had a feeling she wouldn't appreciate the joke.

'Don't touch me!' Patsy said as Mo and I approached her. 'And don't sit down. You'll jiggle me.'

'Why is she in my bed, Mommy?' Mo asked, quick to respond to Patsy's irritability.

'She's going to sleep here tonight, Mo, and you're going to sleep with Kathleen,' Mother said.

Mo stuck out her lip and gave Patsy an ugly look. 'I don't want to sleep with Kathleen. I want to sleep in my bed right here in this room!'

Remembering what Aunt Doris had said about helping, I picked Mo up and swung her around. 'You'll love sleeping in my bed, Mo Mo! I'll tell you stories and sing you songs and tickle your toes!'

To my relief, Mo laughed. 'Spin me more, spin me more!' she shouted. 'Faster! Faster!'

As I galumphed around the room with Mo, thinking how helpful I was being, Rosie followed us, squealing, 'Me too! Me too!'

'Kathleen, for God's sake!' Mother said sharply. 'Stop it! You're getting them too worked up. They'll never settle down.'

'And you're giving me a headache,' Patsy whined.

Red-faced, I lowered Mo to the floor as Mother said, 'You haven't even changed your clothes. Mo shouldn't be running around in her bathing suit.' Taking Rosie's hand, Mother said to Mo, 'Come on, let's get a bath.'

'I was just trying to help.' I followed Mother down the hall, feeling tears well up in my eyes. Couldn't I ever please her?

'Give me some real help then,' Mother said sharply. 'Put them in the tub and let me get some rest.'

Without another word, Mother walked

back to her room and slammed her door shut, leaving me standing in the bathroom with Rosie squirming in my arms.

As I watched the tub fill, I told myself that Mother wasn't really angry with me. She was just upset about Patsy's sunburn, that was all. After she rested awhile, she would be in a better mood.

'Look at me.' Mo stood up in the tub and pointed at her stomach. 'I still got my bathing suit on, only it's white, and you can see right through it!' She laughed and flopped down in the water, nearly swamping Rosie in the wave she created.

Rosie looked at her own little body, still the same pinky white all over. 'Where my bathing suit?'

'You have to go out in the sun to get one,' I told her.

'You?' Rosie pointed at me. 'Where yours?'

'Under my T-shirt.' I cupped my hands and dumped bathwater down her back, making her squeal with laughter.

As Mo launched a series of splashes at Rosie, Mother opened the door and frowned at me. 'Kathleen! Don't let them carry on like that. They're getting water all over the floor. Sit down, Mo, before you fall and hurt yourself!'

The door slammed shut, leaving the three of us alone. Mo giggled, but Rosie looked at me, her lip puckered. 'Where Mommy?'

'Mommy is taking care of Patsy,' I said gently and lifted her out of the tub. I cuddled her on my lap as I dried her, breathing in the sweet clean smell of her skin.

'Come on, Mo, time to get out.' I pulled the plug and Mo sat in the tub, watching the water swirl slowly down the drain.

'Why is Mommy always so cross?' Mo asked as she let me wrap a towel around her. 'She gets mad at everything, just like Daddy.'

I shrugged. 'She has a lot on her mind, Mo.' I hugged Rosie. 'Don't worry about it.'

'Well, I think she's an old meanie, and I don't like her anymore.'

I sighed and handed Mo a towel. What could I say? Mother really was getting awfully hard to get along with. 'Maybe she isn't feeling well,' I said slowly, thinking again about what Aunt Doris had said.

Wrapping her towel around herself, Mo

swung her hips like a hula dancer. 'She better get well soon,' she said as she swayed back and forth. 'Or I'm going to run away to Hawaii. Patsy can come with me, but not you. You're an old Gloomy Gus.'

Sticking out her tongue, Mo ran out of the bathroom, and Rosie followed her, leaving me to mop up the floor while I pondered the unfairness of everything. Didn't anybody appreciate me?

Feeling unhappy and misunderstood, I filled the tub almost to the rim and sank into the water, letting it lap up under my chin. My hair floated out like brown seaweed and my knees stuck up like mountain islands. The bathroom was so quiet that I could hear birds singing outside in the trees.

Green light filtered in through the leaves pressing against the screen, and shadows danced on the walls and ceiling. I felt as remote from the sounds downstairs as a princess in a tower. Like Lady Elaine, I was waiting for Lancelot to ride by in his shining armor.

'Kathleen!' Mother rapped sharply on the door of my chamber. 'Don't you think you've been in there long enough? There's

only one bathroom, you know, and somebody else might need to use it.'

'Yes, Kathleen!' Mo howled. 'Let me in!
I got to go!'

Wrapping myself in a towel, I opened
the door and swept past them. 'It's all
yours,' I said to my sister.

10

The next morning, Fay's friend Cindy showed up while we were washing the breakfast dishes. Like Fay, she wore a lot of makeup, but she was short and dark, and her hair was long and straight. 'You a Colts fan?' she asked, taking in my T-shirt.

'It's my father's.' I concentrated on the plate I was drying. 'He gave me a whole bunch of stuff when the Colts left Baltimore. He's a Redskins fan now.' I blushed as I went rambling on and on. I was sure Cindy didn't care what football team my father liked or why.

She tugged at her bathing suit, a purple one like Fay's. 'You almost ready to go?' she asked.

As Fay let the water out of the sink, Aunt Doris looked up from the newspaper. 'You go along with them, Kathleen,' she said.

Fay flashed her mother a nasty look, but the message in Aunt Doris's eyes was clear. Take Kathleen or stay home.

'I promised Mo I'd go with her later,' I said uncertainly.

'Well, I'm sure Fay won't mind having Mo come along.' Aunt Doris fixed Fay with one of her looks.

Before Fay could open her mouth, Mo bounded into the kitchen with Mother right behind her, carrying Rosie.

'Let's go, Kathleen!' Mo seized my hand excitedly. 'Rosie's coming too. Mother said she could!'

Mother handed me Rosie. 'Keep a shirt and hat on her and put plenty of sunshield on her face and legs. I don't want you bringing her home burned to a crisp like Patsy.'

'Have a good time, you-all.' Aunt Doris somehow got us out the door in a group. Ignoring the scowl on Fay's face, she waved and smiled and shut the screen door firmly behind us.

'Can I carry her?' Cindy stretched out her arms to Rosie. 'I just love kids.'

Fay looked totally disgusted. Huffing

in exasperation, she said, 'Well, at least Patsy won't be coming with us for a while.'

'Yeah,' Cindy said. 'I hear she got a bad sunburn.'

I nodded. 'She's spending the day in bed.'

'Poor thing,' Cindy said, without actually sounding very sympathetic. I supposed Fay had told her every detail of Patsy's behavior at the beach. Turning her attention to Rosie, she blew on her neck and made her laugh. 'You're just adorable, you know that?'

Judging from the expression on Fay's face, I thought she might throw up if Cindy continued to gush over Rosie. 'Listen, it's the Wrecking Crew.' She turned her radio up and waved it at Cindy. 'Aren't they great?'

Cindy nodded, but she was too busy playing 'This Little Piggy' with Rosie to give Fay the attention she wanted.

'Is Joe going to be at the beach?' Mo tugged at Fay's arm to get her attention.

Jerking away from Mo's hand, Fay scowled at her. 'What's it to you?'

'I just wondered,' Mo said, ready to flare up like a Fourth of July rocket. 'Me and Patsy like him.'

'Swell,' Fay said. 'Maybe you'll remember not to say anything else about him to my mother.'

'I forgot he was a secret,' Mo said. 'But I remember now.'

'Good for you.' Fay turned her radio up even louder and stalked ahead, passing Cindy without a word.

When we got to the snack bar, Fay spread her blanket in the usual place. Since it was Monday, we had the beach almost to ourselves. Two old ladies, their backs to us, stood knee-deep in the water talking to each other, and several mothers lay on the sand, gossiping and occasionally telling their kids to stop throwing sand or fighting or whatever. A man with a big dog walked past, and sea gulls squabbled over french fries and other delicacies left by the weekend crowd.

After slathering my sisters with lotion, I told them they could play at the edge of the water while I read.

'Aren't you coming with us?' Mo grabbed my hand and tried to pull me up. 'Mommy said I can't go out to the raft unless you come with me!'

'Not now, maybe later.' I pulled my

hand free. 'Play with Rosie for a while, okay?'

'But she's a baby!'

Fay rolled over on her stomach and buried her face in her arms. 'Does she have to whine like that? Take her out to the raft and drown her before she drives me crazy.'

Cindy laughed. 'Come on, Fay. She's just a kid. Don't be so hard on her.'

Fay mumbled something I couldn't hear, and Mo made a hideous face at her before turning to me with another plea.

'If me and Rosie play now, will you take me later?'

Hoping it might rain or something, I nodded, and she ran down to the water's edge with Rosie toddling behind her.

The minute I opened my book, though, Fay grabbed it and examined the cover. 'Tess of the what?' she squinted at the title.

'The D'Urbervilles. It's by Thomas Hardy.' As soon as I said that, I felt really dumb. Hardy's name was right there on the cover. Fay could read it herself.

Fay studied the picture of Tess. 'Is it any good?'

I nodded. 'It's sad though.'

'Wasn't that a movie?' Cindy asked. 'I think I saw it on cable TV. She kills her old lover and the blood drips through the ceiling and then she runs away with this other wimpy guy. Doesn't she get executed or something?'

'Yes,' I said, glad that I'd seen the movie too. Otherwise Cindy would certainly have ruined the book for me.

'It sounds good, but it's too long for me.' Thrusting the book at me, Fay fluffed her hair with her comb, rolled her eyes at Cindy, and laughed as if she'd said something very witty.

While I read, Cindy and Fay lay on their backs, eyes shut, and baked in the sun like a pair of steaks on a grill. I looked at them a couple of times to assure myself they were still alive. I would have died of boredom lying there with nothing to do.

Finally Cindy sat up and poked Fay. 'Shouldn't Joe be here by now?'

'He said he might have guard duty.' Fay stretched. 'Want to get a Coke or something?'

'Yeah. It sure is hot.' They got up and tugged their bathing suits into place, top and bottom. 'Coming with us, Kathleen?' Cindy asked.

I shook my head. 'I have to watch my sisters.' I squinted across the beach at Mo and Rosie, who were contentedly digging holes near the water's edge.

'If Joe comes while we're gone, tell him to meet us at the snack bar,' Fay said, without bothering to look at me.

'Sure.' I bent my head over my book, anxious to get on with the story. I'd gotten to the part where Tess was about to meet Alec again, and I knew perfectly well what was going to happen, but I hoped the book would be different. It's the same with *Romeo and Juliet* – no matter how often I see it or read it, I always tell myself that Juliet will wake up in time, and they'll live happily ever after.

Before I'd read far enough for Tess to ruin her life once again, a shadow fell across the page, and I looked up. There was Joe, grinning down at me.

'Hey, Smiley,' he said, 'where's your cousin?'

'She wants you to meet her at the snack bar,' I said.

Instead of walking off to find Fay, Joe sat down on the blanket next to me and peered at my book. 'That looks like the kind of stuff they make you read in

98

school,' he said. 'You got a summer reading list or something?'

'No, I just like to read.' I wanted to say something clever, to smile and be interesting, but all I could do was stare at the words on the page. With Joe sitting so close, they looked as if someone had changed them into Latin. I couldn't make sense out of any of them.

'You must be pretty smart. I bet you get straight A's in school, don't you?' Joe grinned at me, and I decided he looked like Laurence Olivier when he played Heathcliff in *Wuthering Heights*, one of my favorite old movies. He had the same squarish jaw and a cleft in his chin.

'I always get C's in P.E. and B's in music,' I said.

'But all the rest are A's, even math and science?'

'I guess so.' I tried to smile at him, but the sun was in my eyes, and I felt all squinty and ugly.

'You and my kid sister, Louise. She's a little older than you, fourteen, but she's a real brain too. In fact, she's got all the smarts in our family. I just barely made it through high school. My little brothers are still kind of young, but they don't like school much.' He laughed and looked around the beach. 'Where's Reds today?'

'Home. She really got sunburned yesterday.'

'Poor kid, but it's her own fault. She should've put that sunshield on like you said.' Spotting Mo and Rosie, he asked, 'Is that little bitty kid part of your family too?'

'That's Rosie. She's almost two.'

'Four girls – doesn't your old man get lonesome?'

I shrugged. 'He's got his brother. They go fishing and hunting and all that.'

'Guess he just has to get away sometimes, huh?' Joe laughed. 'You know, though, a big family's real nice. I keep telling Fay how lucky she is you-all are here. I miss my family a lot, especially Louise.'

While I was trying to imagine Fay's response to this, I heard Mo shriek, 'Joe! Joe!'

'Hey, you little stinker!' He shouted as my sister threw herself at him. Picking her up, he swung her round and round, then dumped her, laughing and begging for more, on the blanket.

'Me too, me too!' Rosie stretched her

chubby arms toward Joe, and he swung her, while Mo grabbed him around the waist and tried to trip him.

As the three of them tussled, Fay strode up to Joe. 'Well, it's about time you got here.' She frowned at him, her hands on her hips, the very image of Aunt Doris.

'Hey, get off, you two.' Still laughing, Joe pulled himself away from Mo and Rosie, who were giggling and clinging to him like barnacles.

'Take me to the raft, take me to the raft, please, Joe, please?' Mo chanted while Rosie sang 'Me too, me too.'

'When you get tired of playing, let me know.' Fay sat down with her back to Joe.

Catching the nasty edge in her voice, Joe squatted down next to Fay. 'It's like being home,' he said. 'They remind me of my little brothers.'

'Do you want to fool around with them or be with me?' Fay's voice rose shrilly, and she stood up and started walking down the beach.

Somehow Joe managed to escape from Mo and Rosie. We all watched him follow Fay along the edge of the water. Even from the rear she looked angry, and I could tell Joe was apologizing to her.

Cindy lit a cigarette and sat down next to me. 'Fay's going to lose him if she keeps that stuff up. He's not going to put up with it forever,' she said glumly. 'I told her a million times she acts like a spoiled brat, but she just won't listen to me.'

I nodded, and we both watched Joe put his arms around Fay and kiss her. Suddenly I wanted to leave, to be anywhere but here where I had to watch Joe and Fay. Nervously, I started gathering up our beach stuff. 'We have to go home now,' I told Cindy. 'I'm worried about Rosie's skin. She's getting kind of pink.'

Cindy turned on Fay's radio and stretched out on her stomach. 'See you tomorrow,' she said.

'Come on, Rosie.' I scooped her up and turned to Mo. 'I think we better get going.'

To my relief, Mo agreed without making a big fuss. As we walked away, I looked back once just in time to see Joe pick up Fay and run into the bay with her. She was kicking and screaming, but I could tell she wasn't really mad. Especially when he lowered her gently into the water and kissed her for the umpteenth million time.

11

As soon as we got home, Patsy insisted I tell her every single thing that had happened at the beach.

'You can't imagine how bored I've been,' she said when I was finished. 'All I did was lie on the glider with a dumb little fan blowing on me. I hate it here!'

'When can you go with us again?' I asked her. 'It wasn't much fun without you.'

'Probably not till next week. Just look at my blisters.' She turned around and pulled her nightgown off her shoulders. 'They're as big as jellybeans,' she said proudly.

I shuddered. Maybe having dull brown hair wasn't so bad after all. At least I'd never have a back that looked like my sister's.

'Look who's coming,' Patsy said. 'The great one herself.' She opened the screen door and ran down the steps.

Fay was washing the sand off her feet at the spigot. She looked up and frowned when she saw Patsy. 'What do *you* want?'

'How are your lips today?' Patsy asked.

'I beg your pardon?' Fay stared at Patsy with all the warmth of a freezer full of ice cream.

'Doesn't kissing make your lips sore?' Patsy leered at Fay. 'Or are they all toughened up by now?'

As Fay raised her arm threateningly, Patsy ran inside. 'You better not hit my sunburn!' she yelled from the safe side of the screen door.

Just as Patsy probably intended, Aunt Doris appeared behind her. 'Fay,' she called, 'get in here and act your age. I could use some help with dinner.' As she spoke, she looked at me, suggesting wordlessly that I too make myself useful.

Suddenly remembering her sunburn, Patsy vanished upstairs, claiming she needed to lie down for a while, and Fay and I found ourselves setting the table together.

While Aunt Doris made lots of noise

banging pots around and running water, Fay muttered, 'You better keep that kid away from me, Kathleen. I'm going to murder her, I swear it.'

I laid a spoon down neatly beside a knife. 'I don't have any control over Patsy.'

'How about Mo and Rosie then? You can at least stop them from pestering Joe all the time.' She banged the salt and pepper shakers down in the middle of the table. 'He's not going to think they're cute much longer. Not the way they act.'

The first day Patsy was allowed to go to the beach again, I was sitting on the sand at the water's edge playing castles with Rosie. Mo and Patsy were out in the bay jumping off the raft, and Fay and Cindy had gone to the snack bar to wait for Joe. It was one of the hottest days of the summer, and the little waves tickling the soles of my feet were as warm as bathwater.

My T-shirt hung on me, trapping heat inside of it, but I couldn't bring myself to take it off or to venture deeper than my knees in the murky Chesapeake. If only I had a nice figure like Fay's, I thought, and a daring personality like Patsy's how different everything would be.

Sighing softly, I concentrated on shaping a tall tower out of damp sand while Rosie dug a moat around the wall she'd built. Let Patsy and Mo risk having their legs bitten off by sharks, let Fay kiss Joe till her lips got sore. Why should I care what they did?

'Hey, Smiley, how's things?'

I looked up, squinting in the sun, and saw Joe grinning down at me. I shrugged and patted the sides of the tower, trying to ignore his long brown legs. 'Okay,' I said.

'Just "okay"?' He squatted beside me and ruffled Rosie's hair. 'How come everything is always *okay*? Isn't anything ever *great* or *wonderful* or even *very nice*?'

I shrugged, not knowing what to say and poked a doorway into the side of the tower. Just as if she sensed I needed a distraction, Rosie chose that moment to sit down on the castle. 'All fall down!' she shouted gleefully.

'Rosie, look what you did!' I said, turning away from Joe. 'Aren't you sorry?'

She laughed and threw herself at Joe. 'Swim me, swim me!' she shouted.

Picking up Rosie, he swished her back and forth in the water. Out on the raft, Patsy and Mo spotted him. 'Joe! Joe!' they shouted. 'Come out here!'

Ignoring them, he looked at me. 'How come you're not out there with those two?' he asked. 'I never see you in the water. You either got your nose in a book or you're playing with Dimples here.' He swung Rosie around and put her on the sand next to me. 'Don't you ever have any fun?'

'I don't know how to swim!' I glared at him, angry that he would say something like that.

'You don't need to know how to swim to get out to the raft. That water probably isn't up to your shoulders. Come on, Smiley, take off that shirt, and we'll go see what old Patsy's up to.' He took my hand and tried to pull me to my feet. 'You scared of getting your hair wet or something?'

'Leave me alone!' I jerked away from him so hard that I almost fell down. Grabbing my sister, I held her tightly against my chest as if she were all that stood between me and disaster. 'I have to watch Rosie!'

'Cindy'll watch her.' He looked over his shoulder. Fay and Cindy had returned from the snack bar, and they were sitting on the blanket, Cokes in hand, staring at Joe and me. As usual, Fay had a mean expression on her face. 'Hey, Cindy,' Joe called. 'Come here a minute.'

Giving Fay a puzzled look, Cindy walked toward us. 'What do you want?' she asked Joe.

'Watch Dimples here for a while.' Taking Rosie from me, he handed her to Cindy. 'I'm giving Smiley a swimming lesson.'

Before I realized what he was going to do, Joe picked me up. Like a groom carrying a bride across the threshold, he ran out into the water. 'Watch out, everybody, watch out!' he yelled. 'Here comes Smiley!'

'Put me down! Put me down!' I screamed. Squirming and kicking, I tried my best to get away from him, but he only gripped me tighter. An old lady jumped out of his way, startled, and a little boy tried to trip him, but nothing could stop Joe. When the water was waist-deep, he flung me into the bay.

Down, down I plunged into the yellow

green water, feeling the bay fill my mouth with a flat, salty taste. Then my bottom hit the muck and sand, and I shot back up, coughing and choking as my head popped out into the sunshine. Knowing exactly how Fay felt when she fell off the pier, I flailed about, looking frantically for jellyfish, expecting crabs to attack my feet and a bluefish to bite off my toes.

Although I didn't see a sign of a shark or anything else, I heard Patsy and Mo out on the raft laughing and cheering. 'Yay, Joe!' Patsy shouted. 'Yay, Kathleen!'

'See? It's not so bad getting wet, is it?' Joe was standing several feet away laughing. 'Cools you off real good, Smiley.'

I glared at him, too angry to say anything. I wanted to tell him that he was a big bully and not nearly as nice as I had thought he was, but I could feel tears gathering in my eyes, and I didn't want him to know he could make me cry.

'Aw, your shirt got all wet. Is that what you're mad about, Smiley?' Wading toward me, he stretched out his hand. 'Give it here. I'll take it back to the blanket for you. By the time you go home, it'll be dry.'

'I'll take it back myself!' I started toward the shore, taking big steps, terrified that I was going to step on something that bit, pinched, or stung.

'No, Kathleen, stay and play with me and Patsy!' Mo bobbed up beside me in the water. 'Let me stand on your shoulders and jump off, like we used to in the pool.' She grabbed at me, trying to climb up my back. 'Stand still, Kathleen!'

'Yeah, play with your sister, Smiley.' Joe reached out and caught hold of my T-shirt.

'Let me go!' I was crying now and I pulled away hard, stretching my T-shirt between us. 'Let go!' For a second, the T-shirt held me. Then I staggered away, free, and lost my balance. When I stood up, I realized that the neck band was all that remained of my T-shirt. Joe was holding the rest of it.

'Oh, look what you did!' Mo shrieked at him.

'Hey, Fay,' Patsy yelled. 'Joe loves Kathleen so much he ripped her shirt off!'

Before I could sink into the bay and drown, Joe started toward me. He was laughing till he saw my face. 'Hey, Smiley, what's wrong? Are you crying?'

'Go away!' Frantically I tried to swim to the raft, thinking I could hide under it till they went home, but Joe was faster than I was.

'What's the matter?' he asked, grabbing me before I could escape.

'Nothing!' I struggled to get away. 'Just let me alone.'

'Come on up on the raft.' Somehow he managed to get me up the ladder. 'You two, go away for a while,' he said to Patsy and Mo. 'Kathleen and me want some privacy.'

'Fay's watching,' I heard Patsy giggle.

'So you better not kiss her,' Mo added.

'Go on,' Joe said. 'Get out of here. I'll buy you a Coke or something later.'

I heard them laughing and splashing away. Then it was all quiet. The water lapped under the raft and rocked it gently up and down. Overhead a gull cried. Next to me, Joe shifted his position and cleared his throat, but I wouldn't look at him or anything else. I sat hunched up, my face on my knees, my arms hugging my legs.

'What's so bad about getting thrown in the water?' Joe asked. 'Or getting your T-shirt torn? If you like, I'll get you a big

U.S. Navy one like I got Louise. She loves it.'

I didn't say anything because I was crying.

'Hey, stop that, Kathleen, I mean it.' Putting his hand under my chin, he tried to make me look at him. 'Tell me what's wrong.'

'I can't,' I sobbed.

'How about if I guess?' he asked me. 'How old are you, twelve?'

I nodded.

'When Louise was your age, she wouldn't go swimming either. At first I thought she was turning into one of those girls who hate to get their hair wet. You know, Fay's kind of like that. I always have to throw her in or she'd just sit there talking to Cindy or listening to her radio.' He smiled at me.

'Then I figured out what was really bothering Louise. All her girl friends had better figures than she did, and she didn't want to go to the pool anymore.'

I knew he was waiting for me to say something, but I wouldn't even look at him. It was awful to know I was so easy to understand.

'You know what? Louise is fourteen

112

now, and she looks great.' He patted the bony wing of my shoulder blade. 'Give it some time, Smiley. You'll be a beautiful girl one of these days. Just cheer up a little, okay?'

I shook my head, and two big tears plopped down on the raft. I knew I'd be skinny and weird-looking all my life, and nobody would ever like me.

Joe sighed. 'You're real cute right now, you know that? If you'd just smile at people, Kathleen, and laugh sometimes.' He stood up, and I felt the raft rock under his shifting weight. 'You want to go back to shore with me? Fay's looking awful grumpy. You know how she gets sometimes.'

I shook my head again.

'You aren't going to sit out here and sulk all afternoon, are you? I told you I was sorry about the T-shirt, but, if you ask me, you look a hundred times better without it. Now cheer up, and remember what my old man used to say, "Laugh, and the world laughs with you; cry and you cry alone".'

The raft bounced up and down as Joe splashed into the water. Lifting my head a tiny bit from my knees, I watched him

113

swim back to shore. A few more tears dribbled down my nose as I thought about what he'd said. If only I were fourteen right now – no, eighteen – and, like Louise, I looked great. Then maybe I'd be the one he was kissing, and Fay would be sitting out here all by herself wishing she were me.

12

I don't know how long I would have stayed on the raft if Patsy hadn't swum out to see what I was doing.

'Joe told me to tell you to stop acting like a baby,' Patsy said. 'He said he was sorry and he's getting you a navy T-shirt, so quit sulking.'

She leaned toward me, and I felt water drip from the ends of her braids onto my back. 'I'm not mad, and I'm not sulking,' I said without lifting my head from my arms. 'Why don't you just go away and leave me alone?'

'You know what Fay said?' As usual, Patsy ignored my wishes and stayed where she was, forcing me to wiggle away from her dripping hair. 'She wanted to know if Joe liked you better than her because you're skinny and she's fat.'

I propped myself up on my elbows and stared at Patsy. 'That's the stupidest thing I've ever heard. You must be making it up.'

Patsy grinned. 'I wouldn't lie. She was really mad at him for sitting out on the raft with you. Guess what he said to her!' Patsy started laughing. 'You'll love this, Kathleen. "You know what, Fay?" he says, "Sometimes you act like you aren't more than thirteen or fourteen yourself." ' Patsy laughed so hard, she started snorting. 'You should have seen her face, Kathleen. I thought I'd die!'

I sat up and pulled my knees tightly against my chest. 'Do you think I look dumb?'

'What do you mean?' Patsy looked at me critically, her eyes narrowed, her head tilted to the side.

'In a bathing suit. Do I look awful?'

'You mean because you haven't got a big chest like Fay?' She shook her head, sprinkling me again with water from her braids. 'You look good, like a model or something.'

'Do you really think so or are you just saying that to make me feel better?'

'Oh, come on, Kathleen. Don't act

116

stupid.' Patsy scowled and stood up. 'Let's dive in, okay? We can race to the fence and back.'

'But aren't there things in the water?' I squinted up at her. 'Jellyfish and crabs?'

She shook her head. 'The fence keeps them out. There's nothing to be scared of. Honest.' She wavered a little, trying to hold a diving stance. 'Let's go!'

I stood up and bent over, eyeing the water apprehensively. I'd lied to Joe about not knowing how to swim. Both Patsy and I had been on the swim team at our pool in Baltimore for years, but in that clear water you could see the lines painted on the bottom. And you knew there weren't any jellyfish lurking just beneath the surface waiting to sting you.

'Ready, set' – Patsy looked at me over her shoulder – 'go!'

She dove into the bay, and I followed her, cutting down neatly through the water and swimming upward before my feet had a chance to touch the mucky bottom. We surfaced a few feet apart and started swimming toward the fence, churning the water into a froth around us. Patsy got there first, touched the fence, and sped back to the raft.

'I won! I won!' she yelled as I swam up panting.

'Wait till I get back in shape,' I gasped, pushing wet hair out of my eyes.

'Isn't the water nice?' she asked.

Holding on to the ladder, I stretched my body out behind me and kicked. It was nice after all, I thought, trying not to think about jellyfish and crabs. Better than sitting on the beach, sweating in a T-shirt, playing with Rosie. 'It's not bad,' I admitted.

'So you can't be mad at Joe anymore, right?' Patsy gazed across the water at the beach. 'I guess Fay isn't mad either,' she added.

I looked at our blanket and saw Joe kissing Fay. Turning away, I hid my face from Patsy. Next she would accuse me of being in love with Joe, and I didn't want her and Mo teasing me and carrying on the way they did about Paul. It wasn't true, of course. Joe was much too old for me to be in love with him.

'That must be all Fay knows how to do,' Patsy said scornfully. 'You'd think they'd get tired of it.' She climbed up on the raft. 'Come on, Kathleen, let's race again. Back to shore this time.'

As soon as we got out of the water, Patsy ran across the sand and flopped down next to Joe. 'Do you know how to Indian-wrestle?' she asked him.

Winking at me, Joe said, 'Sure. You want to try me?'

Patsy thrust out her arm, and Fay whispered something to Cindy about show-offs. Joe gripped Patsy's hand. Pretending he couldn't resist her, he let her push his arm down twice, moaning and groaning and getting red in the face.

'Are you faking?' Patsy asked. 'Are you just letting me win?'

'You really want to know?' With no effort at all, he shoved Patsy's arm down so fast she barely knew what was happening. Then he grabbed her and started tickling her.

'Stop! Stop!' Patsy shrieked. 'No, Joe, no!'

'Me too, me too!' Mo threw herself into the fray, and Joe tickled her and Rosie, too.

'Your turn next, Smiley!' He lunged at me. 'Here comes the Tickle Bird!'

'No! No!' I jumped up and ran.

'Leave Kathleen alone!' I heard Fay say sharply. 'She's too old for those dumb games!'

'Nobody's too old for the Tickle Bird!' Joe grabbed Fay and tickled her till I couldn't tell if she was laughing or crying. Then he kissed her, and she clung to him, gasping for breath.

'Let's get our hot dogs and sodas now,' I said to Mo and Rosie. Daddy had sent Mother some money, and she'd given me enough to treat us to lunch at the snack bar.

After we'd gotten our food, we found a nice booth by the window. Craning her neck to see past me, Patsy said, 'Joe and Fay are out in the water kissing. Sometimes I wish she'd drown.'

'Patsy, that's not very nice.' I frowned at her, but I felt pretty hypocritical because I'd been thinking the same thing myself.

She shrugged. 'Then we wouldn't have to see them making out all the time.'

'They love each other,' I said and bit into my hot dog. It tasted awful, and I wasn't sure I could swallow it without gagging.

'So?' Patsy looked at me, mustard and relish oozing out of the corners of her mouth as she chewed. 'I love him too, but if he was my boyfriend I wouldn't act like she does.' Above her swollen cheeks, her eyes watched me, daring me to laugh.

Instead of laughing, I sighed with exasperation. 'You can't be in love with somebody Joe's age. You're only ten years old, Patsy.'

She gazed past me, still watching Fay and Joe. 'Fay's only fourteen,' she said, 'and, besides, I'll be eleven in September.'

'I love Joe too,' Mo said loyally, smiling across the table at Patsy to get her approval.

'He loves *Fay*,' I said.

'He could always stop loving her. They're not married or anything.' Patsy turned her attention to me, her eyes narrowing. 'You love him too, don't you?'

'Of course not!' I felt my face heat with anger. 'He's twenty years old! He's too old even for Fay!'

The cashier stared across the room at me, and I realized I'd spoken a lot louder than I'd meant to. What was I yelling for? Angrily I choked down my hot dog and tried to ignore Patsy and Mo, who were softly chanting 'Kathleen loves Joe' and giggling.

Without really meaning to, I reached across the table and grabbed one of Mo's braids. Yanking hard, I shouted, 'Why don't you shut up?' Picking up Rosie, I ran out of the snack bar, mortified by my own behavior.

Outside the sun dazzled my eyes, and the heat fell on my bare shoulders like flames shooting from a blast furnace. Still carrying Rosie, I walked down to the water's edge and let her dabble her feet in the waves.

In a few minutes, Patsy waded out to me. 'What's the matter with you today?' she asked. 'First you get mad at Joe. Then you get mad at me and Mo. You're really hard to get along with, you know that?'

I turned and glared at Patsy. 'If you and Mo want to throw yourselves all over Joe and make fools of yourselves, go ahead. Just leave me out of it, okay?'

'Who wants to be around a grump like you anyway?' Patsy yelled. Then she stamped off through the water. 'You skinny old beanpole!'

Rosie looked up at me and tickled my face with her tiny fingers. Then she kissed me. 'Love you, love you!' she said, bouncing up and down in my arms.

Swallowing hard so I wouldn't start

crying or anything dumb like that, I smiled at Rosie and gave her a hug. 'Love you too,' I said, glad that I had at least one sweet sister.

By the end of the day, Patsy and Mo and I had more or less made up. Nobody had actually apologized, of course, but we were speaking to each other again in a sort of guarded way. That's the way it is with the three of us. We fight and say awful things to each other, but then, after we get over being mad, we just go on as if we'd never called each other names.

Anyway, there we were – Fay walking slightly ahead of us, Patsy and Mo right behind her, sticking out their flat little chests and wiggling their fannies in an attempt to imitate her, and me bringing up the rear, carrying Rosie.

'Look!' Patsy stopped and pointed at a poster nailed to a telephone pole. 'The Fireman's Carnival is coming on the Fourth of July!'

'It comes every year.' Fay sounded as all-knowing as Aunt Doris. 'They have it in the parking lot on the other side of the snack bar. You can look way across the bay from the top of the Ferris wheel.'

Patsy's eyes sparkled. 'I love carnivals. Are there lots of good rides?'

Fay nodded. 'They have a merry-go-round for kids your age.'

Patsy glared at Fay. 'I wouldn't waste my time on the merry-go-round. I like the scary ones.'

'You think you're so tough,' Fay sneered.

'I'm a lot tougher than you.' Patsy folded her arms across her chest and glared at Fay.

'Is there really a merry-go-round?' Mo danced around them, too excited about the carnival to notice the fight building up.

Fay nodded. 'You and Patsy can ride it all night. Kathleen, too.' Turning her back on us, she flounced up the street, leaving a trail of rock music behind her.

At the dinner table, Patsy told Mother about the carnival. 'Since Daddy's coming to see us that weekend, we can all go together, just like we used to.'

'That might be nice,' Mother said. She smiled at Patsy, but she didn't sound very enthusiastic.

'Oh, Anne, that seems like a lot for you

124

to do.' Aunt Doris looked at Mother. 'Charlie and I can take the girls, and you and John can stay here and relax.'

'No, I want to go with you and Daddy.' Patsy's voice took on a wheedling tone, and she looked at Mother imploringly. 'We'll be like a family again, just us.'

'Yes, Mommy, you have to!' Mo's voice rose shrilly and I saw Uncle Charlie wince as it hit its highest note.

'I don't really like carnivals, girls.' Mother busied herself wiping Rosie's face. 'I'd be just as happy to stay home.'

'But you never go anywhere with us anymore!' Patsy's face got redder as her voice got louder. 'You haven't even gone to the beach with us.'

Mother sighed. 'It's bad for my skin to be out in the sun too much.' Excusing herself, she lifted Rosie out of the high chair and took her upstairs for a bath.

There was a brief silence. Then Uncle Charlie started telling Aunt Doris about a woman who'd driven into the gas station with a flat tire. 'She thought something was wrong with the car,' he laughed. 'She hadn't even thought to look at her tires.'

Leaving him and Aunt Doris laughing over their coffee, Fay, Patsy, and I cleared the table and washed the dishes. Just as we were finishing up, Fay turned to me. 'Don't think I didn't see you fooling around with Joe,' she said. 'Just remember he's *mine*. He thinks you're a nice kid, but that's all.'

Before I could say anything, she left the kitchen. I stared at Patsy, speechless, but she was leaning against the counter laughing. 'She's so jealous, I can't believe it,' she said. 'Does she think she owns Joe?'

I shook my head. In the silence we could hear Fay talking to Cindy on the phone. 'Of course she looks better without that stupid T-shirt, but she's still a stick!'

'Come on, let's go outside,' I said to Patsy. If Fay was going to say any more about me or my figure, I didn't want to hear it.

In a shady corner of the backyard, Uncle Charlie had built an old-fashioned wooden swing, the kind with two seats facing each other and a platform in between. Patsy and I sat down and rocked gently back and forth. The setting sun's beams lanced through the leaves of the trees, dusting the green with gold and casting long shadows across the grass. Somewhere above us, a mockingbird sang, and from the house we could hear Mo shouting she wasn't tired and didn't want to go to bed. Except for her voice, the evening was very peaceful.

'What's wrong with Mother?' Patsy asked suddenly. 'Why doesn't she ever want to do anything anymore? It wouldn't kill her to go to the carnival with us.'

I watched a sea gull fly across the darkening sky. He looked small and lost, a little white speck tossed about by the wind. 'I'm kind of worried about her, Patsy.' Gazing past my sister's head at the line of trees between us and the bay, I told her what Aunt Doris had said about the doctor. 'The thing is,' I concluded, 'I'm not sure Aunt Doris was telling me the whole truth.'

Patsy twisted one of her braids around her finger and stared at me. 'You mean you think she's sick?'

I picked at a little splinter of wood poking out of the armrest. 'I don't know.'

'Oh, it's just being down here,' Patsy said a little louder than necessary. 'If we were back home in Baltimore, she'd be all

right, I know it!' She began pumping the
swing until we were flying over the grass,
going higher and higher. 'Let's see how
fast this old boat will go!'

The wooden supports squeaked alarm-
ingly, and a branch of forsythia whipped
my cheek. 'Stop, Patsy, I feel like I'm
going to throw up!'

'You're such an old poop, Kathleen!'
Patsy slowed the swing and jumped out
before it came to complete stop. 'I'm
going inside before the mosquitoes eat
me up!'

13

I watched Patsy run across the yard, up the back steps, and into the house. It was almost dark now, but the lighted windows did not invite me inside. Enjoying my solitude, I stretched and looked up at the sky.

While I was searching for the Big Dipper, I heard the screen door slam. 'I'm going over to Cindy's for a while,' Fay called to someone inside.

'You're not going anywhere else?' Aunt Doris's shadow slanted down the steps and across the grass as she followed Fay outside.

'Maybe the roller rink.' Fay sounded edgy, and I knew she was afraid her mother was going to make her stay home. 'We're meeting some kids from school,' she added.

'You know I don't like that place. Too many sailors hang out there, just looking for girls like you.'

'Mother!' Fay sounded desperate. 'I'm not interested in sailors. I have my own friends.'

Aunt Doris hemmed and hawed, but finally she said Fay could go if she promised to be home by eleven. 'Not quarter after, not five after. Eleven on the dot,' she said firmly.

After Fay had vanished into the darkness, I rocked the swing gently and imagined myself going to the rink with her. It would be crowded with skaters, and the only lights would be little colored circles spinning across the walls and ceiling and floor. The sailors' uniforms would shine in the darkness, and Joe would be there. My heart beat a little faster when I thought of him. He would ask me to skate, just to be polite because I was Fay's cousin. Then, as he took my hand, something would happen, and he would realize that he didn't like me just as a friend but as –

No, that was ridiculous. Frowning, I pumped a little harder and tried to think about something else, but the smell of the honeysuckle tugged at me, promising something, making me restless.

Again I looked up at the sky. Back in Baltimore the same stars were shining, and the same little moon was floating above my old house on Madison Street. Maybe Paul was sitting on his back steps gazing at the moon too. Maybe he was even thinking about me.

I tried to picture Paul, but, instead of his face, I saw Joe's face. Did he really think I would be a beautiful girl someday? Tilting my head back, I pumped harder, and felt the night air fan my skin. If only this were a magical swing, and it could carry me up to the stars, far far away from Bay View.

'Kathleen?' Aunt Doris stuck her head out the back door. 'What on earth are you doing out there?'

'Nothing.' I let the swing glide to a stop and ran across the damp grass to the house.

'If I'd known you were out there, I'd have told Fay to take you to the rink with her,' Aunt Doris said. 'You must get awfully bored sitting around here every night.'

Picking up the book I'd left on the

kitchen counter, I shook my head. 'I'm a pretty terrible skater,' I confessed.

Aunt Doris frowned. 'You know what your problem is, Kathleen? You spend too much time with your nose stuck in a book. You need to get out and do things once in a while with Fay.'

Edging toward the door, I thought about some of the things Fay and I could do together. I was sure Aunt Doris didn't mean for me to sit on the beach making out with a sailor or sneak off to the skating rink to meet him.

'Now, don't give me that sad look, Kathleen.' Aunt Doris laughed and hugged me against her big soft side. 'You know I can't help saying what's on my mind whether people like to hear it or not. Being a brain is fine, but you need to have fun, too. That's all I'm saying, hon.'

Telling myself that she meant well, I smiled and kissed her good-night. Then I ran upstairs, anxious to get away before she thought of any more advice.

Later that night after Patsy and I had fallen asleep, something woke me up. Lying very still, I opened one eye and saw Fay creeping across the room as quietly as a thief. Glancing at the lighted dial on our clock radio, I realized it was 1:30 A.M. Had she just come home?

Without making a sound, Fay sat down by the window and lit a cigarette. Whenever she inhaled, the cigarette glowed and illuminated her cheek and nose, but never her eyes. What was she looking at? What was she thinking about?

Beside me Patsy mumbled and stirred in her sleep, and Fay glanced at our bed. As she stubbed out her cigarette, I wanted to ask her what it was like to come home, full of secrets, to a dark house where everyone but you was fast asleep. As she stole past me, though, I shut my eyes tightly. I heard the springs creak as she got into bed. Then all was quiet, and I drifted back to sleep, my question unasked and unanswered.

A week passed, then it was the Fourth of July, the day we'd all been looking forward to. Daddy and Uncle Ernie arrived at noon, and Aunt Doris put Fay and me to work helping her prepare a picnic dinner. We were going to have 'a real old-fashioned Fourth, a family celebration,' she kept saying, but something about her tone of voice made me wonder if she really believed it.

133

After all, things didn't look very promising. Fay was pouting because she had to spend the day with us instead of Cindy. Daddy, Uncle Ernie, and Uncle Charlie were out in the middle of the bay fishing and working their way through the case of beer they'd taken with them. Patsy and Mo were sulking in the swing in the backyard because Mother still hadn't made up her mind about going to the beach with us. The only one who seemed truly happy was Rosie. She was sitting under the kitchen table banging a pot and a lid together and singing one of her nonsense songs.

Around five o'clock, Daddy and his brothers came home, sounding almost as jolly as Rosie. They hadn't caught one fish, but they didn't seem to mind. Neither Mother nor Aunt Doris looked very happy as the men staggered around the kitchen, washing their hands and admiring the food we'd spent all day preparing.

'Well, Annie,' Daddy said, giving Mother a big hug, 'are you coming with us?'

I watched her pull away from his clumsy attempt to kiss her. 'I don't know.

134

It's been so hot today.' She sounded a little like Mo, I thought, fretful and whiny.

'It would be good for you to get out of the house for a while,' Aunt Doris said. 'Like I told you, Charlie and I will take the girls to the carnival, so you and John can go on back to the house after we eat. It's real nice down by the bay in the evening, Anne, with the breeze blowing and all.'

'Yes, Mommy, please come!' Mo pulled on Mother's arm.

'Now, Mo,' Aunt Doris said, 'you let your mother make up her own mind. Don't tug on her all the time like that.'

'Come on, Annie.' Daddy tried again to give her a kiss, but his aim wasn't very good. 'That sun sure went to my head today.' He laughed and punched Uncle Ernie lightly in the stomach. 'How about you?'

Uncle Ernie laughed too. 'What we need is another beer.' He opened the refrigerator, but Aunt Doris slapped his hand away.

'You've had enough for a while,' she said. 'That's for dinner.'

'Are you coming, Mommy?' Mo asked again, her voice rising shrilly.

Patsy and I looked at each other, both of us thinking the same thing. If Mother stayed home, she must truly be sick. After all, she hadn't done much except ice the cake Aunt Doris had baked, and it wasn't difficult to walk to the beach, especially now that it was a little cooler.

'Oh, I guess so,' Mother said, 'but only for dinner. I'm not going to the carnival.'

'Hooray, hooray!' Mo grabbed Mother around the waist and gave her a big bear hug.

Instantly Aunt Doris intervened. Pulling Mo away from Mother, she said sharply, 'Don't be so rough!'

Out went Mo's lip. Knowing what was coming, I stepped in. 'Come on, I'll carry you piggyback.' Letting her scramble up on my shoulders, I led the way to the beach, leaving the others to carry the food.

We found a nice spot in a grove of spindly trees and spread out the food – fried chicken, corn on the cob, macaroni salad, tossed greens, sliced tomatoes fresh from Uncle Charlie's garden, pickled beets, relishes, rolls, cheese, bread, and that Maryland favorite, a platter of steamed crabs, bright red and far too fierce-looking for Mo to dare sample. For dessert, we had cake, cherry pie, and watermelon.

Fay moaned about her diet, and Mo complained about the crabs, but they devoured as much as Patsy and I. Even Mother ate like a starving person, which was a good sign, I thought.

'Well,' Uncle Charlie sighed and leaned back from the table. 'That was wonderful, Dorrie.' Then, turning to Fay and me, he added. 'How about you two cleaning up?'

Fay and I heaved ourselves up from the table and began gathering the paper plates. When we'd each filled a grocery bag with trash, we carried them to the garbage can.

Before going back to the table, Fay turned to me. 'I'm supposed to meet Joe at the Ferris wheel at nine o'clock. Can you help me, Kathleen?'

I looked at her warily, flattered by her friendly tone of voice but uncertain about what she expected me to do.

Fay glanced at her parents, but they were laughing at something Uncle Ernie had said. 'Just cover for me if they see you and want to know where I am. That's all.'

'What do you mean?'

'Just say I'm in the ladies' room or something. Use your imagination, Kathleen. You're not that dumb.'

I nodded, but I felt uncomfortable. I didn't want to get in trouble with Aunt Doris or Uncle Charlie.

As I slipped into my place beside Patsy, Aunt Doris said it was almost time to go to the carnival. 'We want to get a good seat at the Bingo table, don't we, Charlie?'

He winked at her and nodded. Turning to Mother, he said, 'Now don't you worry about Patsy and Kathleen. They'll be with Fay, and they'll know where to find us if they need us.'

'What about me?' Mo wailed. 'I want to go too!'

'You've had a long day already, Mo,' Mother said gently.

'But I want to go on the merry-go-round!'

Aunt Doris frowned at her. 'Some little girls need to learn what *no* means.'

'Daddy, you take me!' Mo ran around the table and flung her arms around him, almost knocking the can of beer out of his hand.

'You heard your mother,' he said crossly. 'It's time for you to hit the hay.'

'Just pick her up and carry her home,' Mother said. 'Ernie can take Rosie.'

'You carry me, you carry me!' Mo wept, stretching her arms up to Mother.

'You're much too heavy for your mother,' Daddy said sharply. Picking her up, he walked off into the darkness with Uncle Ernie following him.

Mother turned to Patsy and me. 'You will stay with Fay, won't you?'

I nodded, but I didn't look at Mother. I was sure my eyes would tell her that I was lying.

'Anne, will you come on?' Daddy called, his voice rising impatiently over Mo's wailing.

'They'll be fine.' Aunt Doris gave Mother's arm a quick squeeze. 'Go on with John.'

Mother smiled uneasily. 'Be good,' she whispered and hurried after Daddy and Uncle Ernie.

'Let's go.' Patsy tugged at me. Without looking back to see if I were following her, she ran after Fay toward the carnival.

From the darkness, I heard Daddy say, 'Get a move on, Annie. Ernie and I need a break from all this nonsense.' He said it lightly, but I could hear the impatience, just under the surface.

'You're not going out, are you?' Mother's voice drifted back to me. 'I haven't seen you for three weeks, John. I need to talk to you about something.'

'Hey,' Uncle Ernie said, 'no need for you to go, John, if it's going to cause problems.'

I couldn't hear what Daddy said next. The sound of the waves got between me and their voices. I had a feeling, though, that he and Mother were probably on the verge of a big argument. Ever since Daddy had come back from fishing, Mother had been edgy, and he'd had the look of somebody who is expecting bad news.

Looking toward the string of colored lights outlining the Ferris wheel, I realized that I was standing all alone on the dark beach. I could just make out the figures of Aunt Doris and Uncle Charlie walking slowly, hand in hand, across the parking lot, but neither Patsy nor Fay were anywhere in sight. Anxiously I ran after my aunt and uncle, hoping to find my sister.

14

After catching up with Aunt Doris and Uncle Charlie, I spotted Fay and Patsy waiting for me by the merry-go-round.

'You-all have a nice time,' Aunt Doris said, 'and don't forget to meet us at the Bingo stand at midnight.'

As she and Uncle Charlie disappeared into the crowd, Fay slipped off in the opposite direction.

'Where did she go?' Patsy stared at the people crowding the midway. 'I bet she's meeting Joe.'

I shrugged. 'So what if she is? We'll have more fun without her.'

'But I wanted to see Joe in his uniform.' Patsy stared at a group of sailors talking to some girls at the refreshment stand. 'I bet he looks so handsome. Wouldn't you like to see him?'

'Not especially,' I lied.

Patsy shook her head and sighed. 'Well, what do you want to do then?'

I shrugged. 'I don't care.'

'Will you go on the Himalaya with me?'

I shook my head. 'You know I hate rides like that. They make me sick at my stomach.'

'Oh, come on, Kathleen,' she begged. 'Just one ride won't kill you.'

'No,' I said.

'You're scared.'

I shrugged. No matter what she said, I wasn't going on the Himalaya. I'd seen it before, and I knew how fast it went. I also knew that the riders always screamed to go even faster. 'Here.' I handed Patsy two dollars. 'Buy the tickets and ride on it all you want. But I'm not going.'

Smiling scornfully, she took the money and ran off to the ticket booth.

After Patsy had ridden the Himalaya three times, the Octopus twice, and the Ferris wheel once, she decided that she was hungry. We bought big pink clouds of sticky cotton candy and strolled along the crowded midway.

'I wonder where Fay is,' Patsy said as we watched a grinning sailor put his arm around his girlfriend and give her a kiss.

I shrugged. 'It must be almost midnight. She better show up soon or she's going to be in big trouble.'

Patsy plunged ahead of me, looking to the right and left, pushing her way through the crowd. Suddenly she stopped and gestured for me to hurry up. 'Over there,' she yelled. 'At the goldfish toss.'

Sure enough, there they were. Fay was holding a blue-and-white panda and wearing a garland of crepe-paper flowers around her neck and a pink Robin Hood cap on her head. Looking more handsome than ever in a spotless white sailor suit, Joe was throwing ping-pong balls at a row of goldfish bowls.

Before I could stop her, Patsy ran toward them. 'We have to remind her about meeting Aunt Doris and Uncle Charlie at the Bingo stand,' she called to me.

Just as Joe tossed his last ball at the bowls of fish, Fay saw us. 'What are you doing here?' she asked, making it obvious that she wasn't pleased to see us.

'You're going to be in big trouble if you don't come to the Bingo stand right now. It's nearly midnight, and you know what

Aunt Doris said.' Patsy put one hand on her hip, daring Fay to argue.

'Why do you have to go to the Bingo stand?' Joe smiled at Fay and pulled her close enough to kiss her nose.

She smiled coyly at him, then turned to Patsy, her smile changing abruptly to a scowl. 'Get out of here! Go ride the merry-go-round or something.'

Ignoring Fay, Patsy asked Joe, 'Did you win that big panda at the shooting booth?'

'I sure did.' He folded his arms across his chest and dazzled us all with his big white teeth. 'It was a lot easier to win him than to get one of these goldfish. I can never figure out which way the wind's going to blow. It messes me up every time.'

'I bet I could get one,' Patsy said.

Joe laughed and winked at me. 'It's harder than it looks, kid.'

'I'm not a kid.' Patsy glared at him. 'I'm almost eleven years old, and I'm good at throwing. Back in Baltimore, I used to pitch in the Little League.'

The man behind the counter leaned down and grinned at Patsy. 'You want to try your luck, sweetheart? Three balls for

twenty-five cents.' A gold tooth glittered
when he smiled, and his skin was as wrinkled as a tobacco leaf.

Patsy reached into the pocket of her
shorts and pulled out a quarter. Dropping
it into his money pouch, the man pointed
at a white line painted on the boardwalk.

'Since you're a kid, you can stand
behind that. Good luck.' He grinned at me
and shook his head as if he were taking
money from a baby.

With her toes on the line, Patsy eyed
the bowls carefully. Then, taking careful
aim, she threw the first ball. It went wide
of its target and so did the second. Fay
hooted, and Joe said, 'I told you it wasn't
easy, Reds.'

Ignoring both of them, Patsy stood
very still and stared hard at the bowls and
the little fish swimming round and round
inside them.

'I already threw away a dollar.' Joe
laughed. 'Get it? I *threw* away a dollar.'
He nudged Fay, but she was too busy
glaring at Patsy to notice. 'You can buy a
goldfish in the five-and-ten for a quarter,'
he added more seriously, 'but then you
got to buy the bowl.'

Patsy nodded, but she didn't look at

him. Slowly she drew back her arm and let the last ball go. Lightly it sailed, small and white against the night sky; then it curved down and dropped gently into a bowl. The fish inside swam madly about, astonished to find its home invaded by an alien object, and Patsy jumped up and down, laughing and clapping her hands.

'I did it, I did it!' she crowed. 'I knew I could!'

'Nice throw, sweetheart.' The gold tooth flashed as the carnival man handed Patsy the bowl. Winking broadly at Joe, he added, 'Looks like the little lady beat you, mate.'

'She sure did.' Joe smiled down at Patsy. 'Where did you learn to throw like that?'

Before Patsy could answer, Fay said, 'He let you stand closer. That's the only reason you got one, so don't get too carried away with yourself. You're conceited enough already.'

Patsy glared at Fay. 'I'm not conceited!'

Clapping her hands and pitching her voice into a high falsetto in imitation of Patsy, Fay bounced up and down on her toes. 'I did it! I did it!' she screeched.

'Leave her alone, Fay,' Joe said. 'She's just a kid. Act your age, will you?'

Glaring at Fay, Patsy said to Joe, 'She *is* acting her age. You don't really think she's eighteen, do you?'

'You better shut up!' Fay screamed and lunged at Patsy.

While Joe stared at the two of them, Patsy ducked away from Fay. Using me as a shield, Patsy yelled, 'She lied, she lied! She's only fourteen!'

'I'm going to kill you!' Fay shoved me out of the way and went for Patsy. Grabbing one of my sister's braids, she pulled as hard as she could, almost yanking her off her feet.

As Patsy struggled to get away, she tipped the goldfish bowl. The water slopped out, carrying the fish with it. Bursting into a wail of misery, Patsy dropped to her knees and tried to catch the fish as it flipped and flopped in the sand.

As Fay went for Patsy again, Joe grabbed her arm. 'What's she talking about? You told me you were eighteen, Fay. You didn't lie, did you?'

'Let me go!' Fay tried to twist away from him. She was crying now, and her

Robin Hood cap was slipping down over her eyes. 'Let me go!'

Joe had a hold of both her arms now and was trying to force her to look at him. 'How old are you?'

But she wouldn't answer him. Still crying, she turned her face away from him. 'Leave me alone, leave me alone,' she wept.

Standing there forgotten by everybody, I looked at Patsy. I was hoping she'd realize what she'd done, but she didn't seem to care about anything but the fish.

'Come on, Patsy,' I said. 'Leave it alone. It's dead now.' I pulled gently at her arm, trying to persuade her to stand up. I wanted to get far away from Fay and Joe, and I wanted Patsy to come with me. Maybe if we left them alone, they would work things out.

'Hey, Kathleen.' Joe turned to me. 'How old is Fay?'

Before I could answer, I saw Aunt Doris and Uncle Charlie walking toward us like actors in a slow-motion film. They hadn't seen us yet; their heads were turned toward a man aiming a rifle at a parade of little tin ducks. When the man pulled the trigger and missed, Uncle Charlie turned away, smiling, and looked right at us. At the sight of Fay and Joe, his smile vanished.

While I stood helplessly watching, Uncle Charlie strode up to us. I wanted to warn Fay, but before I could force a single word out of my mouth, he had reached her side. Grabbing her arm, he pulled her roughly away from Joe. 'What's going on here?' he yelled. 'Who is this guy?'

'Daddy!' Fay cried. 'I thought you were playing Bingo!'

Uncle Charlie ignored her. 'Do you know how old my daughter is?' he shouted at Joe.

Shaking his head, Joe backed away. 'She told me she was eighteen, sir,' he said nervously.

By this time, Aunt Doris had gotten a grip on Fay, freeing Uncle Charlie to confront Joe. Stepping closer to him, Uncle Charlie grabbed Joe's tie and pulled his face close to his so they were practically nose to nose. 'You stay away from my daughter,' he bellowed. The veins stood out in his neck, his face was red, and he looked mean and tough.

Joe gulped and nodded. 'Yes, sir,' he

stammered. 'I'm sorry, sir. I really thought she was older.'

'Get out of here,' Uncle Charlie released his grip on the tie so fast that Joe reeled away from him, struggling to keep his balance. 'Before I call an M.P. and get you court-martialed.'

'No, Daddy, no!' Fay cried. Struggling to escape from her mother, she cried, 'Joe, Joe, wait! Don't go!'

But Joe just looked at her sadly over his shoulder and disappeared into the crowd that had gathered around us.

'I hope you're happy now!' Fay screamed at Patsy, but my sister was still crouching in the sand, weeping over the dead goldfish cradled in her hands.

'Let's go home, for Lord's sake,' Aunt Doris said. The skin under her eyes was puffy, and her whole body sagged with fatigue.

'At least let me get my bear!' Fay reached for the panda still lying where she'd dropped it.

'Leave the damn thing there!' Pulling her after him, Uncle Charlie pushed his way through the crowd with Aunt Doris following them.

'Come on, you two,' she called crossly to us.

Picking up the bear, I turned to Patsy. 'We have to go.'

'My fish, my fish,' Patsy sobbed. Still holding him, she yelled at Fay, 'You murdered him! You killed my fish!'

To my surprise, the carnival man put his hand on Patsy's shoulder. 'Don't cry sweetheart, don't cry.' Handing her another bowl, he said, 'Here, take this one. He's even prettier.'

He held out a dirty hand, and Patsy solemnly dropped the dead fish into it. 'I'll take care of this one, don't you worry,' he said, flashing his good tooth again.

'Thank you,' Patsy whispered.

'And you, cheer up.' The carnival man turned to me. 'It's not the end of the world. She'll find another boyfriend before you can say Jack Robinson.'

I nodded, but I couldn't make myself smile, not even to please the carnival man.

'Will you girls get a move on?' Aunt Doris bellowed.

As we hurried to catch up with Aunt Doris and Uncle Charlie, the carnival man yelled, 'Take real good care of that fish, sweetheart!'

15

All the way back to the house, I tried to
stay at least half a block behind Uncle
Charlie, Aunt Doris, and Fay, but no matter how much I dragged my feet, I could
hear almost everything they said.

'You know what guys like that are looking for, don't you?' Uncle Charlie shouted.

'Don't blame it all on Fay,' Aunt Doris
said to him. 'I'm sure Cindy had a lot to do
with it. She's always been a bad influence.'

She turned to Fay. 'All those nights you
spent at her house. Heaven knows what
you were doing or where you went or what
time you came home! Cindy's mother may
not care what she does, but I care what you
do. You won't be stepping out the front
door for the rest of the summer if I have
my way!'

While Aunt Doris and Uncle Charlie

took turns yelling at her and at each other, Fay walked between them, her head bent, her shoulders shaking with sobs. I felt sorry for her and for Joe, too. He wasn't the sort of person Uncle Charlie thought he was; he loved Fay, I knew he did, and he'd truly believed she was eighteen. His heart was broken, too, just like Fay's.

'He was after one thing, Fay! Just one thing!' Uncle Charlie's voice interrupted my fantasy of Joe walking along the beach, alone and sad, thinking, perhaps, of drowning himself in the bay. 'I hope you didn't give it to him!'

'What's he talking about?' Patsy finally looked up from her fish and frowned at Uncle Charlie's broad back.

'*You* know,' I whispered, embarrassed to say it out loud.

'He thinks *that?*' Patsy stared at me, shocked.

I shrugged. 'He's really mad.'

'That's not fair. He doesn't even know Joe.' Patsy glared at Fay. 'It's all her fault for telling him she was eighteen. She's such a stupid fat dummy.'

'If you had just kept your mouth shut, Patsy,' I said. 'Why did you tell him Fay was only fourteen?'

'I was sick of the way she acts.' Patsy peered at her fish still circling the bowl. 'And anyway what difference does it make? It wasn't my fault that Uncle Charlie chased him away.'

'If everybody hadn't been fighting, we'd have seen Uncle Charlie coming, and Fay and Joe could've run off before he saw them.'

'He would have found out sooner or later.'

'Don't you even care? Look at Fay. Her life is ruined.' I paused and stared at my sister. 'And Joe, think how *he* must feel.'

'He should have punched Uncle Charlie, if you ask me.' Patsy stopped under a streetlight and held up her bowl. 'Isn't my fish beautiful? You know what I'm naming him? Joe Finn the Second. You know what happened to Joe Finn the First?'

She scowled at Fay, appearing now under the streetlight on the next corner, still walking like a prisoner between her parents. 'Fish murderer,' Patsy shouted at her.

'Shut up!' I yelled.

Patsy stared at me, surprised, I guess. 'What's the matter with *you?*'

'Don't you realize we'll never see Joe again?'

'What do you mean?'

'If he's not allowed to see Fay, he won't see us either!' I glared at her, tears gathering in my eyes.

'I never thought of that.' Patsy looked as if she were about to cry too.

'Hey, you two!' Aunt Doris yelled at us. 'Get a move on!'

By the time Patsy and I got home, Fay had already gone upstairs. Since neither Patsy nor I wanted another scene with her, we asked Aunt Doris if we could watch 'Creature Feature.'

'Keep the volume down,' she said. 'Charlie and I are going to bed. It's been a long day.' Without another word, she left Patsy and me alone in the living room.

Sprawled on the rug, we watched an old black-and-white Dracula film, while Joe Finn the Second swam slowly round and round in his safe little world.

'You know what I wish?' I asked Patsy during a commercial. 'That we were back in Baltimore.'

'Me too.' She dipped one of her braids in the water and watched Joe swim around it.

'Do you think Daddy will get a job before school starts?' I asked.

'He better. I don't want to go to school here. This kid I met, Chuck, says the sixth-grade teacher is really horrible. Everybody hates her.'

'Aunt Doris showed me the junior high once when we were coming back from the grocery store. It looks like a jail.'

Patsy sighed. 'Well, it's not even the middle of the summer, Kathleen. Daddy's still got plenty of time.'

Before I could say anything else, the movie came back on and Patsy shushed me. No matter how dumb a horror film is, Patsy hangs on every word, so I knew it was useless to try to talk. Instead I sat next to her and worried. She was still too young to realize how quickly a few weeks go by and how long it takes to find a house and move into it.

I guess I fell asleep in front of the television because the next thing I knew Daddy was waking me up and telling me to go to bed. Bending over me, he smelled like beer and cigarette smoke, and I wanted to push him away.

'Where's Patsy?' I asked him as he pulled me to my feet.

'Ernie carried her upstairs,' he said thickly, 'but we couldn't manage you. Legs too long.' Pointing me in the right direction, he added, 'Up you go, Gloomy Gus.'

As I undressed silently in the dark, I heard Daddy bump into something in Mother's room.

'John?' Mother said. 'It's after two. Where have you been?'

'Out with Ernie.' The bed creaked as he lay down. 'I told you.'

'You've been drinking.' Mother sounded angry and upset. 'I can't take much more of this, John. Not on top of everything else.'

'Don't start that, Annie, not now,' Daddy mumbled.

'It's always the same with you,' she said. 'Not now, not now. When can I talk to you?'

'Later. Tomorrow maybe. I told you, it's going to take me a while to accept it. Do you think I'm any happier about it than you are?'

While I stood beside my bed, not daring to move for fear they'd hear me and stop talking, I heard Mo say, 'What? What?' and then start crying.

157

'Now see what you've done!' Mother said crossly. The bed creaked, and I heard her cross the floor to Mo's cot. 'It's all right, honey,' she whispered. 'It's all right. Mommy's here.'

Daddy mumbled something, the bed creaked a few more times, and then all was quiet. Silently I lay down, careful not to disturb Patsy, and closed my eyes. I wanted to fall asleep immediately so I wouldn't have to think about Mother and Daddy, but, of course, I couldn't. For hours, it seemed to me, I stared at the shadows moving gently on the ceiling, wondering why they were so angry with each other all the time.

Downstairs, I heard Uncle Ernie moving around in the kitchen, opening the refrigerator, running water, scraping a chair across the floor. I felt like running down there and telling him to go away and never come back. It was all his fault Daddy was acting this way. If Uncle Ernie weren't always hanging around, Daddy wouldn't have anybody to go out drinking with. Everything would be better.

But, of course, I didn't move. Instead I fell asleep knowing that the best part of the summer had disappeared with Joe.

* * *

By the time I woke up the next morning, Daddy and Uncle Ernie had already left. 'To beat the weekend traffic,' Aunt Doris said, but from the way Mother looked when she went back upstairs, I had a feeling that she and Daddy had quarreled. Patsy had seen them out in the swing, and she was sure they had been arguing.

'All of a sudden, Daddy got up and walked off. Mother started to follow him, but then she just sat down.' Patsy stared at me across the breakfast dishes on the table. 'I think she was crying.'

I poked at my cereal. On the back porch, I could hear Uncle Charlie reading 'Peanuts' to Aunt Doris, but there was no sign of Fay or anybody else. 'Let's go to the beach,' I suggested.

Patsy shrugged. 'Might as well.' Shoving her chair away from the table, she followed me to the sink and watched me wash my dishes. 'We can stop somewhere and get food for Joe Finn,' she said.

As we left the house, I thought I saw Fay watching us from behind the venetian blinds. She was forbidden to go anywhere for a whole week, and I knew she must hate us for being free to leave.

Although Patsy insisted on searching

the entire beach for Joe, we couldn't find him.

'I told you we'd never see him again,' I said sadly.

'If he really loved Fay, he wouldn't let Uncle Charlie scare him away,' Patsy said. 'He'd be waiting here, just praying she'd come along.'

'He did love her, though, he must have,' I said. 'The way he looked at her and kissed her – he wouldn't stop because he found out she was only fourteen.'

'Then why isn't he here?'

'I don't know.' We were sitting on the raft, resting after a race. I shook my head, watching drops of water fly from the ends of my hair.

'Oh, well.' Patsy sighed and stretched out her legs. 'Maybe we'll come down here again some summer, when we're older and sexier, and we'll see Joe. I'll still love him, but you'll be married to Paul, so Joe will fall madly in love with me. I'll be eighteen – *really* eighteen – and he'll be, let's see, twenty-eight. That's not too old, is it?'

I shook my head. 'I don't know about you and Joe, but I'm certainly not planning to be married when I'm only

160

twenty years old. Not even to Paul.'

'What are you going to do?' Patsy chewed on the end of her braid and stared at me.

'I'm not sure. I want to go to college for one thing. And then I want to travel. Maybe I could be an archaeologist and go off to Africa to study ancient ruins. Or I could be a zoologist and study the lions, like the lady in *Born Free*, or the chimpanzees like Jane Goodall.'

Patsy frowned. 'You better get a job then and start saving your money. The way things are going, you'll need to work your way through college.'

'I know.' I sighed and hugged my knees against my chest. 'I just don't want to end up like Mother and spend the rest of my life in Maryland raising kids.'

'Me neither.' Patsy sighed and looked at her legs. 'Did you ever see so many freckles?'

I giggled. 'You could be in the *Guinness Book of Records* for sure.'

'I'm burning up sitting here. Come on, let's race again!'

We dove in, but kick as hard as I could, Patsy got to shore way before I did.

* * *

For the rest of the week, Patsy and I avoided Fay as much as possible. Taking Mo and Rosie with us, we spent most of the time at the beach. Every day, my sisters searched for Joe while I entertained Rosie, but he must have stopped coming. Maybe he was afraid of meeting Uncle Charlie or Aunt Doris. Or maybe he, too, was avoiding Fay.

I couldn't help noticing that he hadn't made any effort to get in touch with her. Two or three times a day, she wept on the phone to Cindy, and once, when she didn't know I was home, I heard her talking to someone at the naval base.

'Well, will you please tell him to call me?' Her voice shook. 'I've called him at least six times. Are you sure he's getting my messages?'

She hesitated a moment, then put the receiver down and ran upstairs. Before I reached the first step, I heard the bathroom door slam, and I knew she'd gone in there to cry in private.

16

Finally Fay's week of confinement came to an end. Although the sky was heavy with gray clouds, it wasn't raining, and I was sure that Fay planned to go to the beach. Patsy and I had agreed to leave the house early, in case Aunt Doris suggested one of her family outings, but we weren't quick enough. On our way out the door, she stopped us and sent us to the sink to wash the breakfast dishes.

When we were almost finished, we heard Cindy running up the back steps. Rapping on the screen door, she called, 'Fay? You ready?'

'Come on in,' Fay called. 'I'll be down in a minute.'

As Cindy stepped into the kitchen, Aunt Doris raised her eyes from her crossword puzzle and gave her a long, hard look. 'Well, well,' she said. 'What are you two planning to do today?'

Cindy fiddled with the strap of her bathing suit. 'Oh, nothing. Just going to the beach, that's all.'

Aunt Doris glanced at Mother and raised her eyebrows. 'That's all, huh?'

Cindy swallowed so hard her Adam's apple bobbed up and down. She sent me an imploring glance. 'Is Fay almost ready?'

Before I could run up to get her, I heard Fay thundering down the steps.

'Let's go,' she said to Cindy.

'Are you going to the beach now?' Aunt Doris asked.

Eyes wary, Fay nodded. 'You said I could.'

'Why don't you take Kathleen with you?' Aunt Doris locked eyeballs with Fay, daring her to say no.

'I'm going later with Patsy and Mo,' I said quickly, thinking I'd get out of it this time. I wasn't about to be trapped again into going to the beach with Fay.

'You spend too much time with those kids,' Aunt Doris said, giving me the famous stare. 'You need to be with girls your own age or a little older. It can't be much fun spending your whole summer baby-sitting, hon.' She glanced at Mother and added, 'Besides, it would do Fay a world of good to be around a sensible girl like you.'

I turned to Mother, but she nodded her head in agreement with Aunt Doris. 'Go on, Kathleen. Don't worry about Patsy and Mo.'

I realized then that Aunt Doris and Mother had planned this. I was to go along with Fay to make sure she didn't meet Joe.

'Well, that settles that,' Aunt Doris said, smiling broadly at the three of us. 'Get your towel, hon, and run along with Fay.'

'Can't I go too?' Patsy headed for the door behind me, but Aunt Doris jumped up and grabbed her arm.

'Not this time. Let the big girls go off and have a nice time. You can take Mo later,' she said in her no-nonsense voice.

I winced as I visualized Patsy's reaction to a remark of this sort and caught the screen door just before Fay let it slam in my face.

'Hold it!' Aunt Doris followed us outside. 'Let's get one thing straight, Fay.

165

You better not talk to any sailors. If I hear one word about you even *looking* at a sailor, you won't leave this house till you're eighteen!'

Fay glared at her mother, then turned her back and flounced down the driveway with Cindy at her side and me bringing up the rear.

'Have fun, Kathleen!' I heard Patsy yell.

All the way to the beach, Fay and Cindy walked ahead of me, whispering to each other. Every now and then they glanced at me to see if I were listening. I wanted to tell them I wasn't interested in their secrets, but I knew they wouldn't believe me.

Feeling unwanted, I sat down on the edge of Fay's blanket and watched her and Cindy lather each other with suntan oil. Lighting a cigarette, Fay scowled at me. 'Look, Kathleen, I know why Mom made you come with us, but if we see Joe, you better keep your mouth shut.'

'I'm not going to say anything.'

'Sure, Kathleen's okay,' Cindy said, eyeing me through a cloud of cigarette smoke. 'It was Patsy's fault, not hers.'

'She could've kept Patsy away from

us – I *told* her to!' Fay glared at me.

'I'm sorry about what happened, Fay, I really am,' I said. 'And I tried to stop Patsy from bothering you. If you hadn't been so mean about the goldfish, she probably wouldn't have told Joe you weren't eighteen.'

'Oh, shut up, Kathleen, shut up!' Fay's eyes narrowed to slits. 'I'm so sick of you and Patsy and all the rest of you! I wish you'd go back to Baltimore where you belong!'

'Do you think we want to be here?' I was so mad I thought I was going to cry.

'Then why doesn't your father get a job so you can leave?' Fay was yelling, and her face was red and ugly.

'He's trying!' I let my voice rise to match hers. 'Jobs aren't so easy to find these days in case you didn't know!'

'All he and Uncle Ernie do is sit around and drink beer. I heard Mom tell your mother he'll never get a job as long as he's got Uncle Ernie to hang around with.'

'That's not true!'

'And your mother's just as bad as he is. She never does anything but stay around the house all day and let my mother wait on her. "Oh, Doris, could you bring me a glass of ice tea, and, while you're up, would you mind doing a few loads of laundry for me? I'm so tired,"' Fay said in what was supposed to be an imitation of my mother's voice.

'My mother's sick!' I screamed at Fay. 'That's why she can't do much around the house. Ask your mother if you don't believe me. She'll tell you!'

'Sick? Is that what you call it?' Fay laughed and turned to Cindy. 'What do you call a nine-month disease that makes you fat and tired?'

Cindy looked at Fay. 'You better stop right now.' Turning to me, she said, 'Don't mind her. She's still upset about Joe, that's all.'

'That's *all*?' Fay shouted. '*That's all*?'

'What are you talking about?' Ignoring Cindy's efforts to intervene, I stared at Fay. 'My mother isn't pregnant!'

'She is so! If you weren't always sitting around with your nose in a book, you'd know it too.'

I shook my head, trying to blink away my tears before Fay saw them. 'She couldn't be pregnant!'

168

'Come out of your ivory tower and face the facts, Kathleen. Your mother's pregnant, your father doesn't have a job, and your family doesn't even have a house.' Fay glared at me.

'You're lying!'

'Why would I lie? I've heard your mother and my mother talking about it lots of times. Don't you ever notice anything?'

'I hate you, Fay!' I wanted to slap her round pink face, but instead, I yelled, 'I'm glad Joe dumped you, I'm glad! It serves you right!' Then, before she could say anything else, I turned and ran away from her.

Dodging the few sunbathers in my way, I concentrated on putting as much distance between Fay and me as possible. She was a liar, I told myself, a big, fat, ugly liar, and I hated her. I never wanted to see her again.

By the time I reached the fence marking the end of the public beach, I was too tired to run any farther. Climbing over a low breakwater, I walked along the narrow strip of sand separating the bay from the marsh. Here, at least, I was alone.

As I walked, I remembered the time

that Danny Higgins told me there wasn't any such thing as Santa Claus. I'd screamed at him, just the way I'd screamed at Fay, but deep down inside I'd known it was true. I just hadn't been ready to hear him say it out loud. I felt the same way now. No matter how much I wanted to believe Fay was lying, I knew she was telling the truth.

Wiping the tears from my eyes, I wondered what was going to happen to our family. As Fay had said, we had no house, no money, and four kids. Now we were going to have a baby. How were we going to manage?

And how was I going to go home and face Mother? She obviously didn't want me to know she was pregnant.

Angrily I hurled a piece of driftwood into the water. For weeks I'd worried about her, thinking she was sick. Now she could worry about me. She could wonder where I was; she could wonder when I was coming back.

I walked and walked, scarcely aware of the gray, gauzy heat and the mosquitoes buzzing in my ears, farther and farther up the beach until I was too tired to take another step.

Collapsing on an old tire, I watched the gray Chesapeake wash up in tired little waves, slap, slap, slappity slap. On the bay's surface, the jellyfish floated, heaving up and down on the swells. There were more of them than usual this summer, Uncle Charlie said, because we hadn't had much rain. It was the worst jellyfish season in years.

Far out on the horizon, I saw a freighter moving slowly beneath the gray clouds toward the Atlantic Ocean. As it crept past me like a toy pulled on a string, I wondered where it was going. Europe maybe or someplace even farther – Africa, New Zealand, Polynesia.

Remembering what I'd said to Patsy about seeing the world, I wished I were old enough to pack my things and go now. I imagined myself leaning against a ship's railing somewhere in the Mediterranean. In my hand was a letter from Aunt Doris telling me Fay was living in a trailer park expecting her fifth baby – 'And her husband out of work as usual.'

That would never happen to me, I told myself. Picking up a stick, I wrote my name in big, elaborate letters on the sand.

'Kathleen Elizabeth Foster,' I whispered, 'is going to be somebody special.'

'What are you doing?'

Startled by the sound of her voice, I turned and saw Patsy. Her upper lip was beaded with perspiration, and her hair was escaping from her braids in curly wisps. She looked as hot and cross as I felt. 'I've been looking all over for you,' she said.

'I was just taking a walk. Is there a law against that?'

'Did you and Fay have a fight?'

'I felt like being by myself for a while.' Turning my back, I added a few more flourishes to my name with a sea gull's feather, hoping Patsy would take the hint and leave.

'Fay said you walked off, but she wouldn't say why.' Patsy squatted beside me and took the feather out of my hand. 'What did she do, Kathleen?'

'I don't want to talk about Fay.' I bent my head and picked at a mosquito-bite scab on my knee.

'You're crying!' Patsy's pointed face grew fierce with anger. 'We're the Foster sisters, remember? We stick together against Fay. If she was mean to you, I want to know about it!'

Brushing the tears out of my eyes, I squinted at Patsy. 'She was just saying how much she hates us living here. That's all.'

Patsy frowned. 'She must've said more than that, Kathleen.'

Lowering my head, I drew circles around my name. 'Well, she told me something we're not supposed to know.'

'Does it have anything to do with Mother?' Patsy sounded worried. 'Oh, Kathleen, is something really wrong with Mother? Is that why you've been crying?'

Concentrating very hard on the design I was drawing in the sand, I said, 'I guess it all depends on how bad you think pregnancy is.'

'What?'

'She's going to have a baby.' I snapped my stick in two and threw the pieces into the bay.

'Who? Fay?' Patsy gasped.

'No, dummy!' I yelled at her. 'Mother! Mother's going to have a baby.'

'But we don't even have a house.' Patsy was too stunned to get mad at me for yelling at her. 'She can't be having a baby, Kathleen. Fay must be lying.'

173

'She heard Mother and Aunt Doris talking about it.' I stared past Patsy at a sailboat drifting along far from shore.

'But she doesn't have a big stomach.' Patsy twisted a braid around her finger. 'She doesn't look pregnant.'

'It takes a while to show.'

Patsy frowned. 'Why didn't she tell us?'

'I don't know. It was awful to find out from Fay. She was so horrible about it. Like we were poor white trash or something.'

'Do you think Daddy knows?'

'I think so.' I remembered the Fourth of July and the quarrel I overheard. It all made sense now.

'Are you going to tell Mother?'

'No!' I scowled at Patsy. 'And don't you tell her either. Let her tell us!'

'You're mad, aren't you?'

'We've worried about her all summer, Patsy, and she hasn't even noticed. She spends all her time talking to Aunt Doris, never to us. Well, I'm tired of it. I don't want to talk to her about anything!'

Patsy looked surprised. And no wonder. I hadn't realized how angry I was

with Mother till I heard the words fly out
of my mouth.

'I'm going to walk farther up the beach.
You can come if you want.' I stood up,
and Patsy followed me. Before we
rounded a curve, I looked over my shoulder. Even from far away, I could see the
marks in the sand where I'd written my
name.

'How much farther do you want to go?'
Patsy asked after we'd walked a long way
in silence. 'It must be way past lunch-
time. Aren't you hungry?'

'No.' I looked at the gray clouds racing
along the horizon. The sky and the water
had darkened, and far off I heard
thunder.

'It's about to pour down with rain,'
Patsy said. 'Let's go home, Kathleen.'

'Go on back if you want to,' I said.
'I don't care if I never see that house
again.'

As I spoke, rain began falling in large
drops. 'We'll get soaked,' Patsy said.

'I thought it didn't matter if it rained
at the beach. You've got your bathing
suit on, haven't you?'

'Don't get mad at me, Kathleen! I

didn't do anything!' Turning away, Patsy walked off, heading toward Bay View.

'Deserter!' I shouted, but she kept right on going, her back ramrod-straight.

The rain fell harder, flying ahead of a wind strong enough to raise whitecaps on the bay. Thunder rumbled closer, and I remembered what Uncle Charlie had told us about lightning at the beach.

'Wait! Wait!' I ran after Patsy.

When I caught up with her, the wind was blowing harder and the thunder was louder. Just ahead of us, an old pier staggered out into the bay, its pilings crooked and its planks listing to one side. 'Under there!' I shouted.

Huddled together under the pier, we watched the storm sweep past us, driving the bay against the shore in two-foot-high waves and splitting the purple sky with jagged bolts of lightning.

'Sorry I got mad at you,' I said softly.

'It's okay.' Patsy smiled at me.

'I just wish I knew what's going to happen to us.'

'Me too.' She shivered as a cool gust of wet wind whooshed past us. Drawing her knees tightly against her chest, she stared at the dark water.

When the storm finally dwindled to a shower, Patsy and I walked slowly back to Bay View. As we passed the place where I'd written my name a dozen times, I noticed that not one letter was left. The rain had washed them all away.

17

As Patsy and I turned the corner a block from Aunt Doris's house, I saw Mo and Mother coming toward us.

'There they are!' Mo ran up to us. 'We've been looking for you!'

'Where have you been!' Mother frowned at me. 'I've been worried to death about you two. Don't you know how dangerous the beach is during a thunderstorm?'

'We were taking a walk,' I said. 'How was I supposed to know it was going to rain?' I kept on walking, not wanted to talk to her or even look at her.

'See? I told you they were all right.' Aunt Doris joined us in front of the house. 'Come on now, everybody. Dinner's ready.'

Although I didn't feel like eating

anything, I had no choice but to sit at the table, right next to Fay, and force myself to choke down enough food to satisfy my aunt.

'Where were you?' Mother asked me again.

'No place. Just walking.' I stared at my plate.

'She's getting to that age, Anne,' Aunt Doris said. 'You have to expect things like this when they get older. Isn't that right, Charlie?'

'Oh, lord, yes,' Uncle Charlie agreed. 'Look at Fay – she's only a couple of years older and just see how she acts. Before you know it, Kathleen will be chasing after the U.S. Navy too.'

At that, Fay slammed her glass down and left the table.

Frowning at Uncle Charlie, Aunt Doris tried to persuade her to come back. 'You haven't eaten half what I put on your plate,' she said.

'I'm not hungry!' Thump, thump, thump – up the stairs Fay went, leaving an uncomfortable silence behind her.

'Did I tell you about the guy who came in the gas station this morning?' Uncle Charlie looked around the table and chuckled. 'Thought there was something under the hood of his car hooting at him. "It must be some godawful big bird, an owl maybe," he says, "I tell you, I'm scared to look."' He paused, overwhelmed by laughter.

'What was it?' Mo stared at him, her fork poised in mid-air.

Still laughing, Uncle Charlie wiped his eyes with his napkin. 'A busted water pump. You ever hear one? I swear it does sound like a bird or something, makes a hooting noise – hoo-ooo-ooo!'

Mo looked disappointed, but everyone else smiled and nodded. Except me. I just sat there, pushing my food around and hoping Aunt Doris would think I'd eaten some of it.

'By the way, Anne.' Uncle Charlie looked at Mother. 'Did you have a chance to talk to John about the job?'

Mother shook her head. 'He hasn't called this week. You know he and Ernie are doing a lot of overtime.'

'What job?' Patsy stared across the table at Mother.

'Oh, one of your uncle's mechanics is quitting at the end of the summer, and he was thinking your father might want the job,' Mother said.

'How could he work down here if we're going back to Baltimore?' Patsy asked.

'Well, that's something to consider.' Mother took Rosie's glass just in time to prevent her from turning it upside down on her plate. 'We'd have to look for a house in Bay View.'

'But you promised we'd go back to Baltimore!' Patsy's voice rose angrily. 'You promised!'

Mother sighed, and Aunt Doris scowled at Patsy. 'You'll live where your parents decide is best!' she snapped.

Picking up her plate, Patsy stalked away from the table. Mo immediately leaped from her chair and ran after her, leaving me sitting there staring at Mother, too angry to say anything.

'I told you not to mention it in front of the kids,' Aunt Doris said to Uncle Charlie.

'May I be excused?' I got up without waiting for an answer and followed my sisters out to the swing in the backyard.

Later that night, I took a bath and went to bed early, determined to avoid everybody. I didn't want to talk to Fay, I didn't want to talk to Mother, I didn't even want to talk to Patsy. All I wanted was to sleep and forget about everything that had happened that day.

Just as I was sinking into a nice dream about going home to Madison Street, I heard the door open and someone cross the room to my bed.

'Are you asleep, Kathleen?' Mother asked softly.

Pressing my eyes tightly shut, I didn't say anything, hoping she'd go away. After all the times I'd tried to talk to her and been pushed aside, why did she have to pick tonight to come looking for me?

Instead of leaving, she sat down on the side of the bed. 'Did you and Fay quarrel today?' she asked.

I pulled away as she tried to brush a strand of hair out of my eyes. 'I'm trying to go to sleep,' I mumbled, pretending to be much drowsier than I really was.

'Patsy was sure Fay hurt your feelings,' Mother persisted. 'Did she say something that upset you?'

'I just get tired of her sometimes, and I wish I was back home, that's all.'

'I think there's something you're not telling me.' Her voice sounded worried.

'So? You don't tell me everything.' I

182

rolled over on my side with my back to her.

'Are you talking about the job?' She ran a finger lightly down my arm. 'I didn't want to say anything till your father and I talked it over.'

'But you know how much Patsy and I want to go back to Baltimore. I'm in the Honors Program, and Patsy's counting on being in Mrs Miller's room with Mary Lou. You can't make us move down here for good, you can't!' I punched my pillow furiously, trying to keep silent about the other thing she hadn't told me.

'Kathleen,' she said, 'I'm surprised at you. This is the sort of behavior I expect from Patsy, not you! Can't I count on you at least to act your age?'

'Will you please leave me alone? I told you I want to go to sleep!'

'All right, if that's what you want, I'll leave.' She got up, but when she was halfway to the door, she looked back. 'I'm very disappointed in you, Kathleen.' Then she was gone, closing the door behind her.

Pressing my fist against my mouth, I kept myself from telling her how disappointed I was in her. As I listened to her footsteps on the stairs, though, I wanted to call her back and apologize, to cling to her and cry and tell her what Fay had told me. I wanted her to tell me it wasn't true, that Daddy wasn't going to take the job at Uncle Charlie's gas station, that we'd be moving back to Baltimore soon and I'd never have to see Fay again. Instead, I buried my face in my pillow and cried myself to sleep.

Several days later, the sky clouded over and it began to rain, trapping us all in Aunt Doris's house. I was sitting on the glider reading *My Life and Hard Times*. I'd picked it because I thought it would be sad, like my own life, but, to my surprise it was so funny I was laughing out loud.

Suddenly the glider creaked, and Mother sat down next to me. 'Thurber used to be one of my favorite authors. Which story are you reading?'

' "The Night the Bed Fell," ' I said without looking up from the page.

'Oh, I remember that one! The crazy grandfather is upstairs and everybody thinks his bed fell, and he wakes up and imagines he's in the middle of a Civil War battle. The police come, don't they?' She laughed.

'How should I know? I'm only on the first page!' I scowled at her, letting her know what I thought about people who gave away the endings of stories.

'Oh, honey.' She smiled at me apologetically. Ignoring my effort to continue reading, she said, 'You know, your birthday's coming up in less than two weeks, and we haven't even talked about presents and things like that.'

Keeping my nose in my book, I said, 'The only thing I want is to go back to Baltimore. My birthday's in August and school starts just after Labor Day. Am I going to be in Oakton Mills or not?'

'You know I can't answer that question, Kathleen.' She shifted her position, widening the space between us. 'Can't we make some plans for your birthday without your dragging Baltimore into it? Everything will take care of itself sooner or later, you know that. Daddy's doing his best.'

'I don't know that!' I slammed my book shut and jumped to my feet. 'And neither do you!'

'You sound just like Fay!' Mother

stood up too. 'If I'd known you'd start talking to me the way she talks to Doris, I would never have brought you down here!'

'I do not sound like Fay!' I shouted. 'And you can forget all about my birthday! Who wants to be thirteen anyway?'

As I started to walk away, Mother grabbed my arm. 'You sit right back down. I want to talk to you, Kathleen.'

'Talk to me? You never have time to talk to me!' As I pulled away, tears filling my eyes, I saw Rosie running toward us with Mo in pursuit.

'I'm the big bad wolf and I'm going to eat you up!' Mo yelled in a deep, gruff voice. 'Grrr!'

'Mommy! Mommy!' Rosie clung to Mother and peered fearfully at Mo, who was leaping about growling and clawing at her.

Sinking back down on the glider, Mother let Rosie scramble into her lap. 'Calm down, sweetie, calm down,' she said.

'Little pig, little pig, let me come in!' Mo climbed up on the glider next to Mother. 'Now, Rosie, you say, "Not by the hair of my chinny chin chin,"' she prompted.

'No, no! Go away, go away, you bad wolf!' Rosie pushed at Mo, who lost her balance and fell off the glider.

As Mo began howling, I said to Mother. 'See? You never have time for me!'

'Come here, Kathleen!' Patsy yelled. 'Your favorite movie's on – *Wuthering Heights* with Laurence Olivier!'

Leaving Mother to settle things with Mo and Rosie, I went into the living room and flopped down on the couch, just at the right moment for Aunt Doris to see me.

'Don't treat the furniture like that, Kathleen!' she said sharply. 'You'll ruin the springs.'

18

A week before my birthday, Cindy went to North Carolina to spend the rest of the summer with her grandmother, leaving Fay with nothing to do. She moped around the house, refusing to go anywhere and arguing with Aunt Doris about everything from what she ate to what she wore.

Finally one morning, Aunt Doris looked at Fay and me washing the dishes together and said, 'Why don't you two go on to the beach? I'll finish the dishes.'

We both stared at her, thinking the same thing probably. We hadn't spoken more than two words at a time to each other since our fight – why on earth did Aunt Doris think we wanted to go anywhere together?

Ignoring our lack of response, she took

the sponge out of Fay's hand and the dish towel out of mine. 'Go on, it's a lovely day. Why waste it sitting inside?'

'I was waiting for Mother to get back from the store,' I said. 'Then Patsy and I were going crabbing with some kids down at the cove.'

'I don't feel like going anywhere. I've got cramps,' Fay whined.

'Look.' Aunt Doris said. 'You two have been mad at each other long enough. It's ridiculous.' Grabbing my hand and Fay's hand, she made us shake. 'Now make up,' she ordered.

Jerking our hands apart, Fay and I scowled at each other. I didn't want to apologize to her – *I* hadn't done anything.

'Sorry, Kathleen,' Fay muttered.

'It's okay,' I mumbled, too surprised to say more.

'See? Wasn't that easy?' Aunt Doris grinned at us. 'Now go on, get out of here for a while.'

Without saying much to each other, we gathered up our beach supplies and left the house. When we were halfway down the driveway, Aunt Doris stuck her head out the back door and called, 'Watch out for the U.S. Navy!' She made it sound as if Joe were a joke now.

'I hate my mother sometimes!' Fay said, looking straight ahead and walking a little faster. 'When I have kids, I hope I remember not to act likes he does.'

'You'd think our mothers had never been our age,' I said. 'They must forget everything.'

She looked at me as if she were surprised to hear me agreeing with her. 'Just wait. The older you get, the worse they act. I'll be so glad when I'm eighteen and I can leave this place.'

'Me too.' I thought about myself on board that ship sailing across the Mediterranean. For a moment I was tempted to tell Fay about my plans for the future, but I wasn't sure I could trust her not to laugh at me.

Fay was silent for a moment. Then she said, 'I really am sorry I was so mean about your mother. I know I wasn't supposed to tell you.'

I shrugged. 'I would've figured it out sooner or later.'

'Did you tell her I told you?'

I shook my head.

'She has told you, though, hasn't she?'

I shook my head again.

Fay rolled her eyes. 'When's she planning on giving you the big news? The day she comes home from the hospital?'

When I didn't say anything, she added, 'I bet that's why your father hasn't been down here for ages. He's probably mad about it.' Fay wafted the blanket down through the air so that it fell neatly on the sand. 'Do you think he'll take the job at Daddy's gas station?'

Sitting down next to her, I took the bottle of suntan oil she handed me and started spreading it on her back. 'I hope not. I want to go back to Baltimore.'

'People don't always get what they want,' Fay said glumly. 'Look at me and Joe. I really loved him, and then your stupid sister had to ruin everything.'

I sighed. 'I'm sorry about Joe, Fay.'

'Not half as sorry as I am,' she sniffed.

As I opened my book, Fay turned on her radio and closed her eyes. Instead of reading, I gazed out across the bay at the dark blue line where the water met the sky. Big white shaving-cream clouds billowed along the horizon, and a fresh breeze pushed foot-high waves against the shore. It was a beautiful day, I thought, and I was glad that Aunt Doris had forced Fay and me to go to the beach together.

Then I saw something that changed everything. Walking toward us, unaware of Fay's and my presence, was Joe. He wasn't alone. Clinging to his hand was a girl with long blond hair and a beautiful golden tan.

Holding my breath for fear Fay would open her eyes and see him, I bent my head over my book. 'Don't look at us,' I prayed to Joe silently. 'Just keep on going.' But my heart was thumping so hard, I was sure he would hear it.

Of course, the very minute Joe passed by, the radio station started fading, and Fay sat up to fix it. I heard her gasp, then felt her clutch my arm.

'There's Joe!' she whispered. 'With another girl! Oh, Kathleen, what should I do?'

'Nothing,' I whispered. 'Maybe he won't see us!' I glanced at him, but he seemed to see nothing but the girl's hair tossing in the breeze. It hurt to breathe when I saw the smile on his face.

'No,' Fay said slowly. 'I'm going to say hi to him.' She stood up and fluffed her hair back from her face. 'Maybe if he sees me again, he'll, well, you know . . .' Her voice trailed off indecisively, but she started walking across the sand.

I knelt on the blanket, watching the distance between Fay and Joe narrow. When she had almost caught up with him, Fay turned and gestured for me to come with her. Although I was sure she was making a terrible mistake, I ran after her.

'Joe?' she called, and he turned around. He seemed startled, as if he hadn't expected her to be at the beach.

'Hey, kid, how you doing?' He smiled stiffly at Fay. 'Long time no see.'

While the blonde stood beside him, her fingers clasping his, Fay said, 'I called you at the base dozens of times, but they always said you were on duty or something. Didn't you get my messages?' Her voice shook, and I knew she was making a tremendous effort not to cry.

Joe kept on grinning as if he were advertising toothpaste. 'I just never had time, kid.' Turning to me, he flashed his big white teeth. 'And what's with the sad face, Smiley? Where's Reds and the little guys?'

I shrugged and looked down at the

sand, at all our feet. Next to everybody else's, Joe's looked big and hairy.

'You always used to have time to call me!' Fay sounded very close to tears.

'Hey, where're my manners?' Joe said a little too loudly. Putting his arm around the blonde, he drew her closer. 'This is Vicki, and Vicki, this is Fay and Kathleen. They're real nice kids,' he said, smiling down at Vicki, who looked pretty puzzled by the whole situation. 'It's a shame old Patsy and the little guys aren't here. Cutest kids you ever saw. Remind me of my family back home,' he went on, still smiling as if his face were paralyzed.

Shaking her head, Fay backed away from him. 'I'm not a kid,' she said, tears spilling down her cheeks. 'You don't even care, do you? You never did!' Turning away from him, she ran down the beach.

'Oh, Fay, come on back here!' he called after her, but she didn't even pause. If anything, she ran faster.

Turning to me, he said, 'You better go after her, Kathleen.'

'Why don't you?' I shouted at him. 'You're the one she wants to talk to, not me!' I stared at him. Never had I been so disappointed in a person in my whole entire life. How could he treat Fay so badly?

'What's going on?' Vicki tugged at Joe's arm. 'What's wrong with that girl?' She looked past me at Fay, a small figure now in the distance.

Joe patted her hand and smiled at her. 'I'll tell you about it later, okay?' Turning to me, he said. 'Just go after her, will you? Tell her I'm sorry.'

I glared at him. 'You don't look very sorry!' Then I chased Fay down the beach, leaving Joe to explain things to Vicki as best he could.

I finally caught up with Fay at the breakwater. She was sitting out on the end, her face hidden in her hands, crying so hard her shoulders shook.

'Fay?' I laid my hand lightly on her arm, but she pulled it away. 'Are you all right?'

She looked at me. More tears slid down her cheeks taking her mascara with them, and her voice shook with sobs. 'Go away, just go away!'

I moved apart from her, but I had a feeling she didn't really want me to leave. So I sat a few feet away and waited for her to stop crying.

Finally she turned toward me. 'How could he treat me like that? I hate him! I hate him!'

Apparently alarmed, a sea gull lifted itself off its perch on a piling several yards away. It squawked loudly as it flew over our heads.

'I thought he loved me as much as I loved him, but now he acts like I'm just some dumb kid,' Fay wept. 'Doesn't he care that I still love him? Doesn't it mean anything to him?'

Not knowing what to say, I watched the waves lapping against the breakwater. I was shocked myself at Joe's behavior. Like Fay, I'd thought he really loved her. It was frightening to think somebody could forget about you that quickly.

'He must hate me,' Fay wailed. 'What did I do to make him hate me so much? What did I do?' Her eyes were all red and puffy, and her face was splotchy and streaked with makeup. I felt so sorry for her that my own eyes filled up with tears.

'Oh, Fay, I'm sure he doesn't hate you,' I said, knowing as I spoke how inadequate my words were. 'He just didn't know what to say. Probably because he feels so bad about everything. And he did tell me to tell you that he was sorry.'

'*Sorry?*' Fay choked on the word. 'That's all he had to say – he was sorry?'

I nodded, thinking myself that *sorry* wasn't very comforting.

'But why didn't he call me? Not even once?' Fay's eyes brimmed with tears again.

'Maybe he was scared your father would answer the phone.'

She shook her head. 'I left messages for him to call me at Cindy's.' She took a deep shuddering breath. 'If he really loved me, he would have called me. He just thinks I'm a dumb little kid.' Hiding her face in her hands, she started crying again.

While I waited for her to stop, I watched the jellyfish floating up and down on the waves. Quite a few of them had washed up on the beach, probably because the bay was rougher than usual. Lying there, with their tentacles tangled and broken, they baked in the sun. The smell was not pleasant.

'Fay?' I asked when I thought she'd finally used up all her tears. 'Do you want to go back? I've got enough money to treat us to Cokes if you want.'

Wiping her eyes, she tried to smile. 'I am kind of thirsty,' she said shakily.

'I don't see you two together very often,' the cashier said as she handed us two large Cokes with plenty of ice. She smiled at us, her fat cheeks wrinkling. 'Are you sisters or cousins?'

'Cousins,' we said together.

'I knew you was related.' She tilted her head to one side and looked us over. 'One's tall and thin, the other's short and curvy, but there's something around the eyes and the mouth, a family resemblance of some kind.' She rang up the sale and dropped my money into the drawer. 'Have a nice day, you-all.'

We sat down in a booth near the back and stared at each other, trying to see what the cashier had seen.

'I never thought we looked anything alike,' Fay said.

'Me neither.' We peered into each other's eyes and then we laughed. 'Well, mine are gray green and so are yours,' I said. 'I guess that's it.'

'And we have one on each side of our nose,' Fay added.

I nodded. 'And we each have a mouth that opens and shuts.'

We were still laughing when Patsy and Mo came running up to us. 'Did you see her? Did you see her?' Patsy asked, pushing her way into the booth beside me.

'Joe's got a new girlfriend!' Mo shouted. 'And she's real pretty!'

Patsy leered at Fay. 'We saw them kissing!'

'Shut up!' Fay leaped to her feet and ran out of the snack bar.

'Oh, Patsy!' I shoved her out of the booth so hard she fell down. 'How can you be so horrible!'

Leaving Patsy there, I ran after Fay, too angry to care whether I'd hurt my sister or not.

The next time Patsy and I were alone together, we were still too mad to speak to each other. We stood at the sink, side by side, washing the dinner dishes. Fay had gone upstairs right after dinner, complaining of cramps, and everybody else was in the living room watching television.

As I handed Patsy the last plate to dry, I said, 'Why did you tell Fay about Vicki? You know how upset she is about Joe.'

Patsy wouldn't look at me. Sticking out her lip, she shrugged elaborately. 'Since when have you cared about Fay's feelings? I thought you were mad at her because of what she said about Mother.'

'We made up.' I stared at her. 'Patsy, can't you understand? It's not right to make somebody feel that bad.'

She fidgeted, refusing to meet my eyes. 'But you and me are the Foster sisters against Fay. What's the matter with you? Do you like her better than me all of a sudden?' To my surprise, Patsy's lower lip quivered a little.

'Of course not. I just don't want you to be so mean all the time.'

'You aren't going to run off with her and leave me with Mo, are you?' Patsy asked. 'I don't want to play big bad wolf with a six-year-old all summer.'

I shook my head. 'We're still the Foster sisters, Patsy. We always will be. We just won't be against Fay anymore. Okay?'

'Okay, but that doesn't mean I like Fay. It just means I don't want you to be mad at me and go off with her.'

I smiled at Patsy and pulled the stopper out of the sink. As the water swirled down the drain, we set up the

Parcheesi board on the kitchen table and invited Mo to play a game with us. I thought she was a little disappointed that Patsy and I had made up, but she was a good sport about it.

19

Although I'd told Mother I didn't want a party on my birthday, she and Aunt Doris had gone ahead and planned a big picnic dinner, and Patsy and Mo had festooned the tree near the table with balloons and crepe-paper streamers. It was a beautiful Saturday, warm instead of hot. A cool breeze ruffled the leaves and bounced the balloons, making Rosie laugh and dance about, trying to catch one.

While Uncle Charlie grilled steaks, Patsy and I sat in the swing keeping an eye on Mo and Rosie. Rocking it gently with her feet, Patsy looked at me. 'Do you think Daddy will come?'

This was the question I'd been asking myself for weeks. We hadn't seen Daddy for so long, and I had told myself over and over again that he would be here today. No matter how angry or unhappy he was about the baby, he wouldn't miss my birthday. Especially this one, my thirteenth, the most special since my first birthday.

'Aunt Doris set places for him and Uncle Ernie,' I said. 'And Uncle Charlie's grilling enough steaks.'

'But it's almost five o'clock. Isn't that when we're eating?' Patsy chewed on the end of a braid. 'He should be here by now.'

'They could be having car trouble.' I scratched a mosquito bite on my elbow and tried not to worry. He'd come; surely he would.

'Did he say for sure?'

I frowned at her and shrugged. 'I don't know.' I didn't want to tell her that I hadn't actually asked Mother. I knew she thought he was coming, and I had decided to let it go at that.

Patsy sighed. 'Here comes Fay,' she said.

'Mom wants you all to sit down. Dinner's ready,' Fay announced and walked back to the table. She never had much to say when Patsy was around.

Slipping into my place, I stared at the

pile of presents waiting for me.

'You open your gifts, hon, and then we'll eat.' Aunt Doris smiled at me.

'Happy birthday, sweetie.' Mother gave me a hug. 'Don't the decorations look nice?'

Barely glancing at the crepe paper fluttering in the breeze, I pulled away from Mother's arm and sat down stiffly. 'How can we eat?' I said. 'Daddy's not here yet.' I looked around the table uncertainly, my eyes drawn to the empty places next to Uncle Charlie.

'Charlie can't keep the steaks waiting, Kathleen,' Aunt Doris said. 'There's nothing worse than a cold steak.'

Trying to smile, I opened my presents as slowly as I could: there was a diary from Mother, a frilly blouse from Aunt Doris and Uncle Charlie, a bottle of perfume from Fay, and a lady made of seashells and pipe cleaners from my sisters. Thanking everybody, I did my best to look pleased and happy as Aunt Doris began heaping food on my plate.

'I knew he wouldn't come,' Patsy muttered to me. 'I think he and Mother are still in a fight. I wouldn't be surprised if they got a divorce and we had to live here forever.'

I stared down at my plate loaded with food I no longer wanted. Please don't cry, I told myself, biting my lip, please don't cry. It's only a dumb old birthday, no different from any other, and it doesn't matter whether Daddy comes or doesn't come.

'Aren't you hungry, Kathleen?' Mother leaned toward me. 'You haven't touched a thing on your plate.'

'Good lord, she's wearing that sad face again,' Uncle Charlie said. 'It's your birthday, Kathleen. How about a nice big smile?' Looking at all of us, he grinned broadly as if he were giving lessons.

'Now, Charlie, when Kathleen feels like it, she'll smile.' Aunt Doris winked at me over an ear of corn and added, 'It's your birthday. Do what you want, hon, and don't pay any attention to him. Nobody has to smile every single minute of their lives.'

Out of gratitude to my aunt, I bent my head over my plate and forced myself to take a few bites of everything. All around me, conversations sprang up, but I ate silently, refusing to let myself look at the empty places. It hurt to think that Daddy hadn't even called to wish me a happy birthday. Had he forgotten all about it?

By the time we'd finished the cake, it was dark, but we lingered at the table, talking softly. Every time the headlights of car swept across the lawn, I held my breath, sure it was Daddy, but it never was.

Finally Aunt Doris stood up and began collecting the leftovers. 'Time to go inside,' she said. 'The mosquitoes are eating me alive.'

While Mother put Rosie to bed, Fay, Patsy, Mo, and I went into the living room. Almost at once Fay and Patsy started arguing about what to watch; Patsy wanted to see a *National Geographic* special about dolphins, and Fay wanted to see a movie about a teenage runaway. When Aunt Doris suggested we settle it by turning off the television, Fay left the room in a huff.

'Watch what you want,' she said, glaring at my sisters from the hall. 'Who wants to sit around on Saturday night watching TV with a bunch of babies?'

As she started to run upstairs, the phone rang. 'I'll get it!' she yelled. 'Hello?' she said eagerly.

Turning to me, Fay thumped the

receiver down next to the phone. 'It's for you,' she said. Then she ran upstairs, every line of her back expressing her disappointment.

As I picked up the receiver, I held my breath, hoping it would be Daddy. Who else would call me here? 'Hello,' I said softly.

'Kathleen? It's Daddy. Happy birthday, honey.' His voice was blurry, and there was a lot of noise in the background. People laughing and talking slowly, music playing, glasses clinking.

'I'm sorry I couldn't get down to see you today,' he went on, 'but Ernie's car is on the fritz again. The battery just up and died on us. Can't afford to get it replaced right now.'

'It's okay.' I tried to sound happy, but my voice didn't sound natural, not even to me. Uncomfortably I twirled the phone cord round and round my finger. 'We had a picnic in the backyard, and I saved some cake for you.'

'You did? Well, thanks, honey. It's nice you thought about me slaving away up here in Baltimore.' He paused, and I wanted to ask him about his job and if he'd found a house, but I didn't have the nerve.

'Hey, Kathleen,' he said, 'I got a present for you, something you'll really like. If Ernie's got the car running next weekend, I'll bring it down to you.'

Before I could think of something to say, I heard a strange voice ask Daddy how long he was going to be on the phone. 'I got to make a call, man,' the voice said.

'Where are you, Daddy?' I asked.

'Oh, Ernie and I are getting something to eat, honey. I'm on a pay phone, so I can't talk very long.' He paused again. 'Is your mother around?'

I looked up the stairs. Mother was about halfway down, staring at me. 'Is that your father?' she asked.

I nodded. 'He wants to speak to you.'

As I handed her the receiver, I thought I heard Daddy say 'happy birthday' again, but I wasn't sure. The people in the restaurant were making too much noise.

While I hesitated at the foot of the steps, Mother looked at me sharply. 'Kathleen, if you don't mind, I'd like some privacy while your father and I talk.'

Embarrassed, I ran upstairs. Did she think I was eavesdropping? 'Excuse me!' I yelled at her from the top of the steps, but she didn't even look at me.

As I stood there scowling down at Mother, Fay opened the door to our room. 'Kathleen, can I talk to you for a minute?' She wiped her eyes, trying to hide the traces of tears.

I followed her into the room and sat down next to her on the bed. Hugging the big panda bear Joe had won at the carnival, Fay stared at me. 'I'm so unhappy I don't know what to do,' she said, beginning to cry again. 'I can't stop thinking about Joe. If I could only see him again, if I could only talk to him, just once.'

While she buried her head in the panda's tummy and wept, I stared at her sadly, wishing I could think of something I could say or do to make her feel better.

Timidly I patted Fay's shoulder. 'Is there anything I can do?' I imagined myself setting up a rendezvous at the old pier or delivering a love letter.

Fay sat up suddenly and gripped my shoulders. 'There is something you can do, Kathleen, but you have to promise never to tell anybody. Can I trust you?'

'Of course.' I tried to sound more certain than I felt. Suppose she really did want me to go the base and talk to Joe? What would I say? What would I do?

As if she sensed my anxiety, Fay said, 'Don't worry. I'm not asking you to help me run away or anything. I just want you to go someplace with me.' She gazed at me imploringly, her eyes shining with fresh tears.

'Where do you want to go?'

'Well, every Saturday night Joe and his buddies get together at this place on Bay Avenue. They never take dates, so I know that girl wouldn't be there.' Fay paused again and took a deep breath. 'Will you go to Uncle Willy's with me?'

I stared at her, horrified. I knew where Uncle Willy's was. We'd driven past it many times on the way to the store or the library. Even in the daytime, sailors and guys on motorcycles blocked the sidewalk and spilled out into the street. Once we saw a couple of police cars parked in front, and Aunt Doris had said that somebody had probably gotten stabbed or shot. I couldn't imagine Joe in a place like that.

'Joe wouldn't go there,' I said.

'All the guys do,' Fay said in her Aunt Doris voice of authority.

'Well, *we* can't.'

'Look, Kathleen, all I want to do is look

in the window. If we see Joe, we'll get somebody to go in and get him.' She sniffed, and a tear or two slid down her cheek. 'Please, Kathleen, please say you'll come with me.'

I hesitated. I didn't want to let her down, but the thought of going to Uncle Willy's on a Saturday night was pretty scary.

'I'll never ask you to do another thing for me, Kathleen, I promise. Just this one time, please help me.' Fay leaned toward me, her tears begging me to say yes.

'You're sure we don't have to go inside?'

'I swear it.'

'And you're sure he'll be there?'

'Yes, yes, I'm positive.'

'Well, I . . .'

'You'll go then?'

'Yes, but –'

Fay threw her arms around me and hugged, squashing the panda between us. 'Oh, thank you, Kathleen, thank you. I knew I could count on you!'

While I wondered if I'd lost my mind, Fay made her plans. We would ask Uncle Charlie if we could walk to the Dairy Queen, something he often let her and

211

Cindy do. Then we would go to Uncle Willy's and look in the windows and find Joe. After he and Fay got everything worked out, he would drive us home, dropping us off at the corner, of course, so nobody would hear the car.

Following Fay downstairs, I hovered in the doorway while she asked Uncle Charlie about going to the Dairy Queen. Luckily he was in the kitchen all by himself, and Mo and Patsy were still watching the dolphin show. Otherwise, I was sure Patsy would have tried to get involved.

'Sure, sure, you can go,' Uncle Charlie said amiably. Putting down his beer can, he reached into his pocket and pulled out a five-dollar bill. 'Since it's Kathleen's birthday, treat her to anything she wants.'

Feeling guilty, I thanked him and sidled toward the kitchen door behind Fay.

'Where do you think you're going?' Aunt Doris's voice came out of the dark and made me jump. I hadn't realized that she and Mother were sitting on the glider.

'Daddy said I could treat Kathleen to something at the Dairy Queen,' Fay said in her sweetest voice. 'We won't be gone long.'

'You be careful walking around after dark in those shorts,' Aunt Doris said. 'Don't you let anybody pick you up.'

'Are you sure they'll be all right?' Mother asked Aunt Doris. 'It's almost ten o'clock.'

'The Dairy Queen's only a couple of blocks away. What could happen to them?' Aunt Doris chuckled. 'You can't hold on too tight, Anne. You have to loosen the apron strings sometime.'

As Fay and I slipped out the screen door and down the steps, I heard Aunt Doris add, 'Isn't it nice to see them going somewhere together?'

20

Outside, the night air was cool on my arms, and a breeze smelling of salt water ruffled my hair. All around me, the locusts shrilled in the trees, and I felt reckless and wild. I was thirteen now, thirteen, and even I didn't know what I might do next.

'Speed it up, Kathleen,' Fay hissed. She was at the end of the driveway, waiting impatiently. 'We haven't got all night, you know.'

As we passed the front of the house, I saw the blueish glimmer of the television in the living room. Wouldn't Patsy be surprised if she were to look outside and see Fay and me gliding like silent shadows down the street?

Fay walked faster, and I almost had to run to keep up with her. On either side of the street, the yards were dark, and bushes and trees cast menacing shadows across the sidewalk. Uneasily I remembered a show I'd seen on 'Creature Feature.' A girl was walking past a tall hedge just like the one brushing against my arm. All of a sudden, the leaves rustled behind her. She looked over her shoulder and saw a werewolf leaping out at her. She screamed and ran, but he caught her. The next thing I saw were her feet slowly disappearing under the hedge.

'Kathleen, will you hurry a little?' Fay was waiting for me on the edge of the Dairy Queen parking lot. Her skin was greenish white in the light of the neon sign, and her lipstick was a purple slash on her face.

As she started to walk past the oasis of safety the Dairy Queen represented, I grabbed her arm. 'Maybe we should just get sundaes and go back home,' I said. All my daring had vanished, and instead of being excited, I was afraid.

'Don't you dare chicken out on me now!' Fay glared at me. 'You promised to go to Uncle Willy's, Kathleen. You promised!'

'I know, but –'

'You *promised!*' Fay said this so loudly that a man waiting in line to buy ice cream for his wife and kids stared at us. 'You know how much this means to me! If you want to run home to Mommy, fine, go ahead; see if I need you!'

Without giving me a chance to say anything, Fay started walking quickly toward Uncle Willy's. I couldn't let her go by herself: suppose she were kidnapped or something? It would be all my fault for leaving her. Wordlessly, I hurried after her.

Pushing and shoving, Fay burrowed through the crowds of sailors thronging the sidewalk. I didn't really catch up with her until she stopped for the traffic light on the corner opposite Uncle Willy's.

'We can't go over there, Fay.' I grabbed her arm and stared across the street.

A big sign over the entrance to Uncle Willy's flashed on and off, outlining wine glasses and dancing girls in red and green neon. Loudspeakers blasted rock music at the crowd of sailors milling around on the sidewalk. Guys on motorcycles roared up and down the street shouting insults at each other and everybody else.

Fay shrugged. 'Wait here for me then, *baby*.'

'But look at those guys.' I pointed at the motorcyclists wearing denim jackets with the sleeves ripped off. Two of them revved their engines a few inches away from Fay and whistled.

'If you ignore them, they won't bother you,' Fay said, folding her arms across her chest and staring straight ahead.

'Let's go home; come on, Fay.' I tried to tug her back from the edge of the curb, but the light was changing.

Shaking me off, Fay started across the street, and I followed her, too scared to wait alone on the corner.

Ignoring a sailor who tried to grab her arm, Fay pushed through the crowd and pressed her face against one of the big plate-glass windows facing the street. Standing as close to her as I could, I peered into Uncle Willy's too. I prayed that we'd see Joe, but it was dark and crowded inside, and all the sailors looked alike in their uniforms.

'Do you see him?' I looked at Fay anxiously.

'Not yet.' She inched along the window, staring past the people sitting in the booths on the other side of the glass. 'But I'm sure he's in there. The minute he sees us, he'll come out and get us.'

'Hey, honey, what's the matter? You lose your boyfriend or something?' A big, scary-looking guy was leaning against the window, blocking Fay's path. A gold hoop dangled from one of his ears, and his sleeveless denim jacket was covered with motorcycle badges.

Without looking at him, Fay tried to step around him, but he didn't seem to notice that he was being ignored. Putting his hand on Fay's arm, he stopped her. 'You're real cute,' he said.

Fay pulled away, stepping hard on my feet in her haste to escape. 'Get your hands off me!' she said, but her voice shook a little.

'Aw, come on, honey. How about a ride on my bike?' He took a big swallow from his beer can and wiped his mouth with the back of his hand.

Fay shook her head and backed away from him. 'Leave me alone,' she said.

'Come on, come on, let's get out of here!' I grabbed Fay and tried to drag her away.

'Who's this?' Earring leered past Fay,

noticing me for the first time. 'Hey, I'm not going to bite you or nothing. I'm a real nice guy, honest I am.'

'Let's go home, Fay, please!' I tugged at her again.

'Dwayne, look here.' Earring turned to a guy sitting on a motorcycle a few feet away. 'Nice, huh?'

Dwayne shut off his motorcycle and swaggered toward us. He gave Fay a long, admiring look and then, at Earring's suggestion, turned to me. 'Is there a funeral going on around here someplace? Where's the hearse, man? Where's the coffin?' He laughed and slapped Earring on the back.

'Want some beer, honey?' Earring put his arm around Fay and poked the can under her nose. 'Come on, loosen up. You're only young once, you know.'

Fay yanked away from him, but we were trapped against the window. I looked inside, desperately searching for Joe, but I didn't see him. All around us, people blocked us, keeping us near Earring and Dwayne.

Shoving Earring as hard as she could, Fay shouted, 'Get away from me! I mean it!'

'What's going on here?' Out of the crowd, which stepped aside fast to give her room, came a woman police officer. 'You two, over here,' said sharply to Fay and me.

Dwayne and Earring immediately disappeared as the officer grabbed Fay and me by the arm and marched us away. I didn't know what she was going to do, but at that moment I was sure I'd rather be in jail than anywhere near Uncle Willy's. Jail had to be safer.

'Name and age.' The officer stopped next to a squad car and frowned at us, a clipboard and pen in her hand. The streetlight above her head shone down on us, casting sharp shadows on our faces, and I wondered if I looked as pale and scared as Fay did.

A group of sailors stared at us as they walked past, and one of them laughed before they disappeared into the crowd still jamming the sidewalk in front of Uncle Willy's.

After the officer had written down our answers to her questions, she shook her head. 'What did you think you were doing hanging around a place like that?' Her voice was so harsh, I was sure she thought we were juvenile delinquents hoping to find some fun and excitement with guys like Earring and Dwayne.

'We were looking for somebody,' Fay whispered. She was staring down at the ground, and I could see tears creeping down her cheeks.

'You sure found him, didn't you?' The officer asked coldly.

'Not him, we weren't looking for him,' Fay sobbed.

'Do your parents know where you are now?' She turned her steely eyes on me.

'Oh, please don't tell them!' Fay cried. 'We'll go straight home, I promise, and we'll never come near this place again!'

The officer sighed and opened the door of the squad car. 'Get in,' she said.

Wordlessly Fay and I slid one after the other into the back seat. The officer closed the door, locking it, I noticed, and got into the front seat.

As the car pulled away from the curb, Fay gasped, 'Are you taking us to jail?'

'It could probably be arranged.' The officer stared at Fay over her shoulder. 'Let's see, I could charge you with loitering and being a public nuisance.'

As we both burst into tears, she said,

'But why don't I take you home instead? I'm sure your parents would love to know where you've been.'

When we pulled up in front of the house, the first person I saw was Uncle Charlie. He was standing on the sidewalk staring at us. Behind him were Mother and Aunt Doris, and behind them were Patsy and Mo peering out the screen door. They all looked as if they expected bad news.

Opening the back door for Fay and me, the officer led us to our parents. Here on the front steps, she didn't look as big as she had on Bay Avenue. In fact, she was shorter than Mother, and the pistol she wore on her belt made her list a little to the side.

'I'm Lieutenant Schwartz,' she said to Uncle Charlie. 'First of all, I want to assure you that Kathleen and Fay have not been harmed, and they are not being charged with any violation of the law.' She paused and fixed her eyes on Fay and me. 'I drove them home because I was concerned about their safety. Uncle Willy's is no place for girls their age.'

'Uncle Willy's?' Uncle Charlie stared at Officer Schwartz. 'They told me they were going to the Dairy Queen, but they were gone so long, I got worried and went down there looking for them. No wonder the girl at the counter hadn't seen them!'

He turned to Fay, his face reddening in anger, but before he could say another word, Officer Schwartz stopped him.

'I'm sure that you, as responsible parents, will see that Kathleen and Fay stay away from Uncle Willy's.'

'We certainly will.' Uncle Charlie's voice shook with anger and embarrassment. 'I hope you don't think that these girls come from homes where nobody cares what they do.'

As I listened to Uncle Charlie thanking Officer Schwartz for bringing us home, my stomach churned. What would happen to Fay and me after the policewoman left? I was afraid to look at anyone, but as Officer Schwartz walked past, she patted me on the shoulder. 'Buck up, kid,' she said. 'They aren't going to kill you.'

21

The minute the squad car's taillight vanished, Uncle Charlie started yelling. Without letting us explain anything, he accused Fay of lying and sneaking around and humiliating him. Every time he paused to take a breath, Aunt Doris would throw in a few words about Fay's selfishness and irresponsibility.

As soon as she had a chance to escape, Fay ran into the house and up the stairs. 'I wish I was dead,' she screamed from the top of the steps. Then her door slammed. In the sudden silence, we stood in the hall and listened to her crying.

Uncle Charlie muttered something about female hysteria and vanished into the kitchen, leaving me alone with Mother and Aunt Doris. I wanted to run up the stairs after Fay, but as I put my foot on the bottom step, Aunt Doris turned to me.

'Maybe *you* can explain what you and Fay were doing at Uncle Willy's,' she said.

'We were looking for Joe,' I said. 'Fay thought he'd be there, but we couldn't find him, and these other guys started bothering us.'

'Joe?' Aunt Doris frowned. 'That sailor Fay was with at the carnival?'

I nodded. 'She *loves* him.' I looked at my aunt then, wishing I could make her understand how important Joe was to Fay.

'Loves him?' Aunt Doris stared at me. 'That's ridiculous. She's only fourteen years old. What does she know about love?' She looked at Mother and sighed. 'Maybe I better go up and talk to her.'

As she climbed the steps slowly and heavily, Uncle Charlie walked past me, beer in hand. Glancing upstairs, he shook his head and went into the living room to join Mo and Patsy in front of the television set. Folding my arms tightly across my chest, I leaned against the wall and stared at my feet. If only Rosie would start crying and make Mother forget about me!

But, of course, I wasn't that lucky. Out of the corner of my eye, I saw Mother step toward me. 'I want to talk to you, Kathleen,' she said. Taking my arm, she led me out to the kitchen.

Without speaking, we sat down across from each other at the table. Under the overhead light, every flaw in Mother's skin was magnified – the pores in her nose, the fine lines radiating outward from the corners of her eyes, the beginning of creases bracketing her mouth. Wearily, she pushed her hair behind her ears and stared at me. 'What's going on, Kathleen?'

'Nothing.' Blinking hard, I gazed down at the table's pink surface. No matter how much I wanted to, I was not going to break down and cry in front of her.

For several seconds, she was silent. Without raising my head, I shot a quick look at her, then dropped my eyes before she saw me. Finally she said, 'I thought you were such a sensible, responsible girl, Kathleen. How could you lie and deceive me like this?'

I shrugged and concentrated on examining the fake-marble swirls in the tabletop.

'I don't understand,' Mother said, her voice rising a little. Reaching across the table, she tilted my chin up to make me look at her, but I pulled away so fast I almost turned my chair over.

'Leave me alone!' I yelled, and then the tears started splashing down my cheeks whether I wanted them to or not. 'I'm not a baby anymore!'

Mother drew back. 'What's the matter with you, Kathleen? Why are you acting like this?'

'I'm tired of being sensible, I'm tired of it! All summer long, I've taken care of Mo and Rosie and tried to help you, but you've never even noticed.' I paused and covered my face, trying to hide my tears. I wanted her to make me stop, but she didn't say a word.

'All you do is criticize me!' I yelled. 'Sometimes you act like I'm all grown up, and other times you treat me like a baby. I can't stand it!'

'What are you talking about?' Mother was staring at me as if I were a complete stranger.

'You know how important the Honors Program is to me, you know how much being in Mr Goldfein's English class means to me. But I don't know where we're going to be living when school

227

starts. You won't tell me anything!'

'I don't know anything *to* tell you, Kathleen!' Mother brushed her hair out of her face. 'It's not my fault, it's your father's. Ask *him* where you'll be going to school, not me!'

'How can I ask him? I never *see* him!'

She shook her head and leaned on the table, her body sagging. 'I can't tell you what I don't know.'

Words I didn't want to say filled my mouth like stones. 'But you do know you're pregnant! You could have told me that!' I put my hand over my mouth, but it was too late. The stones had hit their target.

'How did you find out?' she whispered.

'Fay told me. She was mad because of Joe, and she made it into a joke. Why didn't you tell me? Why didn't you?'

'Oh, Kathleen, she must have heard me talking to Doris about it.' Mother sighed and sat back down. 'It's been such a bad pregnancy. Doctor Ibarra was afraid I was going to miscarry at first, so it seemed pointless to tell you girls.' She sighed and tried to smile at me.

'When I saw him last week, though, he said everything was fine.' She wound a strand of hair around her finger the way Patsy does when she's uneasy about something. 'I was going to tell you all soon, but I didn't think the news would make anybody very happy. This isn't a very good time to be pregnant, is it?' She smiled at me, silently asking me to understand.

'I thought you were sick; I thought you had cancer or something.' I stared at her, remembering how scared and worried I'd been.

She shook her head, making her hair swirl around her shoulders. 'No, it's just another baby. Maybe it will be a boy this time. You'd like a little brother, wouldn't you?'

'That would be nice for Daddy, I guess.' I tried to work a little enthusiasm into my voice. 'Just so we wouldn't have to name him after Uncle Ernie.'

'No. I've already told your father the closest I'll come is Michael Ernest.' She smiled again, more naturally this time. 'He's due on January third. Maybe he'll come early and be a New Year's baby.'

'But suppose Daddy hasn't found a job by then? What will we do?' Although I wanted to be happy, I couldn't help worrying. As Mother herself had said, it wasn't a very good time to be pregnant.

'I don't know,' she said softly, all the life going out of her voice. Her head was lowered, her face hidden by her hair. 'I just don't know.'

Edging slowly toward her, I laid my hand lightly on her arm. 'Do you think Daddy will go to work for Uncle Charlie?'

She sighed. 'I haven't been able to get him to answer one way or another, Kathleen. He's so upset about everything.' She put her arms around me and drew me down on her lap. 'Try not to worry about it, sweetie. Something will work out, I'm sure of it.'

I leaned against her shoulder, feeling the familiar hardness of her collar bone under my cheek. Stroking my hair, she asked me if I would be upset if we found a house in Bay View instead of going back to Baltimore.

Sadly I thought about Mr Goldfein and the Honors Program and all the other things I loved about Baltimore, including Paul. 'I'll miss my school and my friends.'

Mother nodded. 'I'll miss Baltimore too, but it's cheaper to live here, Kathleen. Daddy won't be earning a lot of money working for Uncle Charlie, but it'll be better than it is now. At least we'll all be together in our own house.' She paused. 'And if the steel plant starts rehiring, we can always move back. Living here might just be temporary.'

I pulled her arms around me more tightly and breathed in the fragrance of shampoo still clinging to her long hair. 'I'm sorry I lied about going to Uncle Willy's,' I said.

'And I'm sorry I didn't tell you about the baby before Fay did.' She hugged me.

I stared at the white hand she rested on my dark knee. There were so many questions I would have liked to ask her about the new baby: Did she really want it? Was Daddy still mad about it? But I had a feeling they weren't the kind of questions parents answered truthfully. At any rate, Uncle Charlie came into the kitchen before I had a chance to say another word.

'Never saw such long legs,' he said, looking at the two of us. 'Must be like holding a colt on your lap, Anne.'

Mother smiled and held me tighter while I stared at my legs splayed out in front of me like knobby bamboo poles. I was sure my uncle thought it was silly for me to sit on my mother's lap, and I wished he hadn't picked this moment to come looking for a beer.

As he opened the can, Uncle Charlie said to me, 'If Fay ever asks you to go to Uncle Willy's again, Kathleen, you say no. Then come tell me or Doris about it. Just suppose Lieutenant Schwartz hadn't come along – there's no telling what might have happened to you girls. It makes my blood run cold to think about it.' Shaking his head, he went back to the living room.

Mother sighed and gave me a gentle shove. 'I think my lap's had it for tonight, honey. Let's go see what your sisters are doing.'

Mo was curled up on the couch sound asleep, and Patsy and Uncle Charlie were watching *The Bride of Dracula*. They glanced at Mother and me and made shushing noises as I bent down to pick up Mo.

'No, no!' Mo kicked and screamed, her eyes shut tight.

'Come on, Mo, bedtime,' I said as I carried her upstairs.

Leaving Mother to undress Mo and get her into bed, I tiptoed into Fay's room, hoping I wouldn't wake her. After what we'd been through, I was sure she needed her sleep.

A few minutes later, Patsy crept into bed next to me. 'Tell me everything, Kathleen,' she whispered.

'Oh, Patsy, not now.' I yawned to show her how tired I was. 'Wait till tomorrow.'

'Now, Kathleen. I want to know *now*.' Her jaw jutted out, and I knew she'd never let me go to sleep till I told her every detail, so I sighed and began to summarize the night's events.

Although Patsy was disappointed that Joe hadn't rescued us, she loved my description of Dwayne and Earring. 'You should have taken me with you. *I* wouldn't have been scared!' she said. 'Those jerks, I'd have kicked them where it hurts!'

She also envied my ride in the squad car. 'Weren't you sorry Lieutenant Schwartz didn't turn on the siren and the lights?'

I shook my head, thinking Patsy might have felt differently if she'd been with Fay and me in the backseat of that car.

'How about Mother? I heard you-all

yelling at each other.' Patsy's eyes sparkled. 'Was she really mad at you?'

'Not really.' I gazed at the shadows dancing about on the ceiling, arranging and rearranging themselves in endless patterns. 'I told her I know about the baby.'

Patsy sucked in her breath. 'What did she say?'

'That everything would work out, that we might have to live down here for a while, but maybe we could move back to Baltimore if the steel plant starts rehiring.' I yawned again, wanting desperately to go to sleep. It seemed that this day, my birthday, had been going on forever.

'And you think that would be okay?' Patsy sat straight up, her voice rising. 'You must be crazy, Kathleen!'

'Mother said we'd all be together in our own house, Patsy. Isn't that what's most important?'

'Not in a house in Bay View. A house in Baltimore!'

'Shut up, you two!' Fay sat up, draped in sheets, and scowled at us. 'Can't I ever have my peace and quiet?'

'Now see what you did,' I snarled at Patsy. 'Do you have to be such a loudmouth?'

'You dumb old simpy-simp jellyhead!' Patsy flopped down and turned her back to me. 'Who wants to talk to you anyway?'

She tossed and turned, jabbing me every now and then with a bony knee or elbow, but she finally relaxed and lay still, leaving me to stare into the darkness, wide-awake. In the distance I could hear the waves washing against the shore. 'Shush, shush, shush,' they seemed to say. 'Wait till you're grown, wait till you're grown.'

22

Fay and I were grounded for a week as a punishment for going to Uncle Willy's. To keep us from getting bored, Aunt Doris put us to work cleaning the house. We washed all the windows inside and out, vacuumed upstairs and down, rearranged and organized closets and drawers, painted the basement walls, and scrubbed the kitchen and bathroom floor. At the end of the week, our hands were red and peeling, but the house was spotless.

Saturday morning, we were finishing up our last chore – cutting the grass and weeding the flowers – when we heard a car turn into the driveway. It was Daddy and Uncle Ernie, all smiles, despite the gray clouds.

'Well, well,' Daddy called as I ran

across the lawn to meet him with Mo and Patsy close behind me. 'Look at my girls!'

'Daddy! Daddy!' Mo flung herself at him and squealed with pleasure as he picked her up and gave her a big hug.

Lifting her over his head, he spun her round and round while she laughed and begged him to go faster.

'Careful, John.' Mother watched him apprehensively. 'She just ate three doughnuts.'

'No, no, don't stop!' Mo cried as Daddy lowered her to the ground.

'That's all for now.' Freeing himself from Mo, Daddy pulled something out of his pocket and smiled at me. 'I know it's a week late, honey, but happy birthday anyway.' He held out a small box wrapped in tissue paper.

'Oh, Daddy, you didn't have to get me anything.' I took the present from his outstretched hand and fumbled with the ribbon. Finally I managed to rip the wrappings apart and open the box. Inside was a small watch with a digital face and a silver stretch band.

Daddy smiled at me uncertainly, his head tilted to one side, his hands thrust into his pockets. 'Do you like it?'

I nodded. 'It's beautiful,' I whispered as I slipped it on my wrist. I glanced at Mother to see if she thought he'd spent too much, but she smiled at me over Rosie's head and then bent down to say something to Mo.

'It's a good watch,' Daddy said proudly. 'Don't wear it to the beach, though. It's not waterproof.'

I smiled at him, wanting to give him a hug and a kiss but afraid of embarrassing him. 'I love it, Daddy, and I promise I'll take good care of it.'

Patsy grabbed my wrist and stared at the watch. 'When I'm thirteen, I want one just like it,' she told Daddy.

'Me too, me too!' Mo danced up and down, tugging at Daddy.

'You can't even tell the time,' Patsy said.

'When I'm thirteen I'll be able to, dumbhead.' Mo stuck out her tongue at Patsy and then followed Daddy and Mother toward the house. 'Daddy, Daddy, will you spin me some more?' she asked, grabbing at his hand.

Daddy took off his baseball cap and put it on Mo's head. 'You run along with Kathleen and Patsy now,' he said.

Turning to me, Mother said, 'Take Rosie for a while, honey. Go to the beach or something, okay?'

'But we haven't got our bathing suits on, and it looks like it's going to rain,' I protested.

Mother followed Daddy into the house and let the screen door close between us. 'Just go on, Kathleen. We have a lot to talk about,' she said.

As Fay pushed past me to open the screen door, Aunt Doris blocked her path. 'You go along with Kathleen and the others,' she said.

'How come?' Fay frowned at Aunt Doris.

'You heard your mother,' Uncle Charlie shouted from the kitchen window.

Muttering to herself, Fay flounced down the steps and followed Patsy, Mo, and me down the driveway.

'You girls on your way to the beach?' Uncle Ernie looked up from the fishing tackle he was sorting and grinned at us. 'Have a nice time, and don't let the jelly-fish bite.'

'They don't bite,' Mo said scornfully. 'They sting with their long horrible tentacles.' She waved her arms and wiggled her

239

fingers at Uncle Ernie as if she were a jellyfish about to attack.

'Isn't Daddy going fishing with you?' Patsy asked.

Uncle Ernie shrugged. 'He's got business to discuss with Charlie first. Maybe later we'll get some fishing in.'

'It's about the job, isn't it?' Patsy frowned at Uncle Ernie.

'That's none of your beeswax, is it?' Uncle Ernie tested the swing of his fishing rod and slammed the trunk shut. 'See you guys later,' he said and set off down the street toward the pier, walking too fast for us to catch up with him.

Luckily he didn't look back. If he had, he would have seen Patsy stick out her tongue and make a horrible face at him. 'I hate Uncle Ernie,' she muttered.

'He's no worse than any other adult,' Fay said. 'At least he's good-looking. Too good-looking for his own good, my mother says. But what does she know?'

'Not much,' Patsy agreed, but she said it so softly Fay didn't hear. In a louder voice, she added, 'Daddy's going to accept that job, Kathleen. I know it.'

I shifted Rosie from one hip to the

other. 'Maybe it won't be so bad, Patsy. He won't be living with Uncle Ernie anymore.' I paused and looked at her. She was shuffling along the sidewalk, head down, scowling at her feet. 'I don't think he and Mother are still mad at each other,' I said in a low voice.

Patsy sighed. 'Good old Pollyanna, that's you.'

'Can me and Patsy go swimming?' Mo asked. 'We got our bathing suits on.'

'Go ahead,' I said as Fay spread the blanket on the sand. 'But don't blame me if you get pneumonia.'

As Patsy and Mo splashed into the cold gray waves, I found a plastic spoon for Rosie so she could dig holes. Then I sat down next to Fay and watched the breeze stir up little whitecaps all the way out to the horizon.

'I love your watch, Kathleen,' Fay said.

'Thanks,' I said, pleased that she liked it. 'It's the first present Daddy ever got me. On Christmas and all my other birthdays, the cards always said *Love, Mother and Daddy*, but I know Mother picked out everything.'

Fay nodded. 'It's the same at our house. Except the year I got a bicycle. I know Daddy bought that. He wouldn't have trusted Mom to get it.'

'Don't you feel sorry for your parents sometimes?' I stared at Fay, trying to see her face through the flying strands of her hair.

'What do you mean?' she asked. 'What's so sad about my parents?'

'Not just your parents, Fay. Everybody's parents. Adults in general, I guess. Sometimes their lives seem so sad.' I paused, wanting her to understand what I was trying to say. 'They must have wanted more when they were our age. Now they seem so trapped with children and houses and jobs and all that.'

Fay pushed her hair out of her eyes and gazed out across the bay at the gray clouds streaking the sky. 'I'm not going to end up like my mother, that's for sure,' she said.

I sighed and picked up a handful of sand. As it trickled through my fingers, it left a tiny shell on my palm. 'Look,' I held it out so Fay could see. 'Isn't it pretty?'

'That's a lady slipper,' Fay said. 'When I was little I used to think they were good luck.'

'But not anymore?'

She shook her head and frowned at the bay spread out in front of us.

'But look, it has a tiny little hole in it. You could put it on a chain and wear it around your neck.'

'So? You could hang an oyster shell around your neck too. It's bigger. Maybe it would bring you even more luck.' She grinned at me to show she didn't think I was completely stupid.

I shrugged and slipped the tiny shell into my pocket, thinking the chance of a little luck was a sufficient reason to keep it. Besides, it was pretty.

'What are you going to do when you grow up, Fay?'

'When I grow up? What do you mean?' Fay lit a cigarette, covering her head with a towel so the wind wouldn't blow out the match. 'I *am* grown up, Kathleen. As soon as I graduate from high school, I'm going to California. I'll get a job and have a really good time for a few years, maybe till I'm twenty-two or three. Then I'll get married, but I won't have kids, at least not right away.' She turned to me. 'How about you?'

'I'm going to college and get a degree in archaeology or anthropology. I'm not sure which yet. And then I'll travel.' I looked at her, hoping she wouldn't think I was hopelessly immature. 'Sometimes I think it would be neat to go to Africa and study chimpanzees like Jane Goodall. She got married while she was there, and she and her husband' – I stopped because Fay was laughing. 'What's so funny?'

'Who did she marry? A good-looking monkey?' Fay laughed so hard she choked on her cigarette smoke. 'Oh, Kathleen, sometimes you're too much!'

Hugging my knees against my chest, I peeked at Fay, trying to decide whether she was ridiculing me or just teasing me. 'I don't see anything funny about wanting to do something different,' I said slowly.

Fay smiled and stubbed her cigarette out in the sand. 'Just send me a wedding announcement' – she giggled – 'and I'll send you a case of chocolate-covered bananas.'

I laughed too, knowing now that she was only kidding me. Stretching out my legs, I watched a sea gull circle overhead, coasting effortlessly on the breeze.

'Hey, Fay!' A tall boy ran toward us

and flopped down on the edge of the blanket. 'I haven't seen you all summer.'

Fay grinned. 'I've been here almost every day, David.'

'Nice life if you can afford it. I'm a working man myself. Got a job at South Shore at the Salty Oyster Carry-Out.' He made a face to show he hated it and looked at me.

'This is my cousin, Kathleen,' Fay said. 'Kathleen, this is David Bennett. We've known each other since I was in kindergarten and he was in first grade.'

David scrutinized my face. 'I can tell you're related,' he said. 'You've got the same eyes.'

I looked at Fay and we giggled. 'One on each side of our nose,' she said.

David smiled at me. 'What grade are you going in?'

'Eighth.' I drew a spiral in the sand, tracing it slowly round and round with my finger.

'Calvert Cliffs Junior High, huh?'

'If we move here. We might go back to Baltimore.'

'Stay here. It's much nicer. Don't you think so, Fay?' David turned back to my cousin.

245

She shrugged. 'I guess so.'

'You want to go to the movies tonight?' David asked her. 'I got my license last week, and Dad's been real nice about letting me use the car.'

'Unless I get a better offer.' Fay smiled at him in a way that suggested only the lead singer of the Wrecking Crew could tempt her to change her mind.

'Kathleen, Kathleen, I'm cold!' Mo splashed out of the water and teetered to a stop at the edge of the blanket. Staring at David, she said, 'Who's he?'

As Fay introduced David to Mo and Patsy, I hoisted Rosie onto my hip. 'We've got to go home, Fay,' I said.

'Tell Mom I'm at the beach with David.' Fay smiled at me.

'I guess she's got a new boyfriend already,' Patsy said as we walked away. 'He's cute too. But not as cute as Joe.'

'No,' I said sadly. 'Not as cute as Joe. But at least we don't have to keep him a secret.'

23

When we were almost home, we met Mother walking toward us. Mo ran to meet her, but Patsy and I hung back. We could tell by the uncertain smile on Mother's face that Daddy had accepted Uncle Charlie's offer.

'He took the job, didn't he?' Patsy glared at Mother.

She nodded and reached out, meaning to hug us. Her smile faded when Patsy pushed past her and ran toward Aunt Doris's house.

'Wait for me!' Mo charged after Patsy, leaving me holding Rosie.

'Let's go for a walk, Kathleen,' Mother said. Without saying anything, we turned back toward the beach.

As the silence between us grew, I shifted Rosie from one hip to the other.

'Do you want to get down for a while?' I asked her.

To my relief, Rosie slithered down to the sand and toddled along the edge of the bay, laughing as the little gray waves washed up over her feet.

'So we'll be living here.' I glanced at Mother from the corner of my eye.

'Doris and I have been looking at houses for a couple of weeks now, and I think I've found one we can afford. It's on the other side of town, up near the north end and so close to the bay you'll be able to see it from your bedroom window. It needs some work, but I'm sure your father and Charlie can get it fixed up so we can move in by October. It's a cute little house.'

She stared at me, holding her hair out of her face. 'Try to talk to Patsy, tell her it won't be so bad down here. She'll make friends soon enough when school starts.'

I nodded, but I turned my head away and gazed out across the bay at the stormy sky. I didn't want her to see the tears beginning to fill my eyes.

'I know you're disappointed, too, Kathleen, but the junior high here has lots of good courses and teachers. You'll like it if you give it a chance.'

I nodded again and sniffed, trying hard to stop the tears from running down my cheeks.

'I can count on you, can't I?' Mother sounded worried. 'I'm going to need you to help when the baby comes. I can't manage all by myself. You know how your father is. He doesn't feel comfortable around an infant.' She laughed uneasily as if she were apologizing for him.

It didn't seem to me that Daddy felt comfortable around children of any age, but I knew I couldn't tell Mother that. 'Sure,' I said, still not daring to look at her, 'I'll help.'

We walked silently, interrupted every now and then by a shout or a laugh from Rosie as she waded a little deeper into the water and then ran back up the beach.

'Let's sit down for a while,' Mother said. Spreading out the full skirt of her dress, she made herself comfortable on the sand. As Rosie scrambled into her lap, Mother put an arm around me and drew me closer to her. 'Just look at those gulls.' She pointed to a half dozen or so, circling overhead, their cries drifting toward us on the wind.

'They look so free, as if they haven't got

a care in the world.' With her face tipped up and the wind in her hair, she looked like Patsy.

'They have to look for food all day,' I said. 'And they fight each other for every scrap they find.'

'But at night, they sleep on the water, and the waves rock them to sleep,' Mother said. 'And when they fly, they rest on the wind and soar over the world. Just think how the bay must look from up so high, all wrinkled and sparkling in the sunlight.'

I picked up a stick and began writing my name in the sand, embellishing it as I had before with flourishes. Without looking at her, I asked, 'When you were my age, what did you want to do when you grew up?'

She sighed and shook her head. 'I don't know. I suppose I had all sorts of silly notions, like most kids do.'

'I bet you didn't think they were silly when you were thirteen.' I frowned and began writing my name again.

'No, I don't guess I did.'

I glanced at her, and she smiled at me through Rosie's curls. 'What do you want to do, Kathleen, when you grow up?' Mother asked.

Uneasily I picked up a handful of sand

and let it trickle through my fingers. Suppose I told her and she laughed as Fay had? 'I don't know.' I shrugged elaborately and watched the sand blow away as it escaped my hands. 'An archaeologist maybe or an anthropologist.'

She bounced Rosie on her knees. 'Once I thought about doing something like that,' she said. 'I wanted to see the world.' She smiled as if she were remembering a foolish idea.

'I'm really going to do it!' My voice sounded so fierce it almost frightened me.

Mother looked away again, out at the storm clouds scudding darkly along the horizon. 'I think if people want something badly enough, they get it,' she said.

I nodded, letting my eyes follow a gull as he flew high into the sky, a flash of white against the dark clouds, leaving the other gulls still circling low over the water. He cried once, sharply, and veered away. I watched him till he was out of sight.

'Well,' Mother stood up and brushed the sand from her dress. The wind flattened her skirt against her stomach, and I noticed how rounded her figure had become. 'Let's start back. I think Rosie's getting tired and hungry. Aren't you, sweetie?'

Lifting Rosie, I walked down the beach beside Mother, following our own straggling footsteps across the sand. The wind was blowing harder now, bringing with it the smell of rain, and there was no one in sight.

'Icky, icky!' Rosie pointed at a jellyfish washed up on the beach.

Mother nodded. 'The jellyfish season is almost over. Labor Day is next week, and then the beach will be closed till Memorial Day.'

'But we'll still be able to come down here for walks, won't we?' I looked at the empty stretch of sand and water, thinking how beautiful and peaceful it was.

'Oh, sure,' Mother said. 'There just won't be any more jellyfish.'

We laughed and turned away from the bay, leaving the gulls squabbling among themselves. A few minutes later, we saw Patsy and Mo playing hopscotch in front of Aunt Doris's house. Rosie twisted out of my arms and ran toward them, eager to be included in the game.

'Look, Kathleen, look what I got!' Patsy waved a postcard. 'It's from Mary

Lou! They're in Ocean City, the lucky ducks. And there's a P.S. for you.'

'What?' I tried to snatch the card, but she giggled and pulled away.

Holding it out of my reach, she read, 'Tell Kathleen Paul says "Hi." '

'Does it really say that? Let me see! Let me see!'

She laughed and handed me the card. Sure enough, there it was, crowded on at the very bottom: 'Tell Kathleen Paul says "Hi." '

'Well, well, will you look at that lovely smile?' Aunt Doris asked. 'That's the happiest I've ever seen you look, Kathleen.'

'Do it more often, and you'll have the boys chasing you instead of Fay,' Uncle Charlie added.

Patsy pulled me toward the house. 'Come on, Kathleen, let's go write a letter to Mary Lou!'

Patsy ran up the steps, and I followed her. Deep in my pocket, my fingers brushed against the tiny lady slipper shell.

THE END

DAPHNE'S BOOK

BY MARY DOWNING HAHN

"How could Mr O'Brien have done such a horrible thing to me?"

Jessica is beside herself when Mr O'Brien chooses her to be Daphne's partner in a school project. All the kids at school hate Daphne and think that she is strange. She wears bizarre, mismatched clothes and never speaks to anyone.

But Jessica is in for a pleasant surprise. As she and Daphne work together, their friendship grows and she discovers the tragic secret that Daphne must keep hidden from the world.

0 552 523046

CORGI

STAR WIND

BY LINDA WOOLVERTON

'Kidsters.'

A calm voice came from the top of the grand lobby staircase and Camden looked up to see a shadowy figure leaning casually against the bannister.

So this was the WT-3 her old friend Mitch had been babbling about, Camden thought. This was the WT-3 who gathered Mitch and the other Kidsters together most days in the dusty, derelict building down in forbidden Venice. This was the WT-3 who talked of trashing the grownies with their muddle-fuddle rules and vacuum-packed minds, and gave the group new, strange-sounding names. Mitch and the others loved it, just lapped it up – especially The Game.

Only Camden had a niggling doubt as she saw the vacant look in her old friends' eyes and heard the harsh, ugly and violent new words. Only Camden began to suspect that there was something rather sinister about the mysterious WT-3 . . .

0 552 52459X

CORGI

If you would like to receive a Newsletter about our new Children's books, just fill in the coupon below with your name and address (or copy it onto a separate piece of paper if you don't want to spoil your book) and send it to:

The Children's Books Editor
Young Corgi Books
61–63 Uxbridge Road,
Ealing
London W5 5SA

Please send me a Children's Newsletter:

Name . . . .

Address . . . .

. . . .

. . . .

All the books on the previous pages are available at your local bookshop or can be ordered direct from the publishers: Cash Sales Dept., Transworld Publishers Ltd., 61–63 Uxbridge Road, Ealing, London W5 5SA.

Please enclose the cost of the book(s), together with the following for postage and packing costs:

Orders up to a value of £5.00	50p
Orders of a value over £5.00	Free

Please note that payment should be made by cheque or postal order in £ sterling.